LOS ANGELES
WITHOUT A MAP

LOS ANGELES
WITHOUT A MAP

RICHARD RAYNER

SECKER & WARBURG
LONDON

First published in Great Britain 1988
by Martin Secker & Warburg Limited
Michelin House, 81 Fulham Road,
London SW3 6RB

British Library Cataloguing in Publication Data
Rayner, Richard
    Los Angeles without a map.
    I. Title
    823'.914[F]   PR6068.A949/

    ISBN 0 436 40550 4

The quotation from *Decline and Fall of the Roman Empire* by Edward
Gibbon, D. M. Low Ed., (Chatto & Windus) is reprinted with the kind
permission of the author's estate, the editor and the publisher.

The quotation from *Sunset Boulevard* is reprinted with the kind
permission of Paramount Pictures (*Sunset Boulevard* © 1949
Paramount Pictures Corporation. All rights reserved).

Every effort has been made to contact the copyright holders of material
used in this book. We will be pleased to make the appropriate
acknowledgement for any ommission in any future edition.

ACKNOWLEDGEMENTS

DURING THE WRITING of *Los Angeles Without a Map* many people gave me encouragement and many others, most generously, volunteered stories about Los Angeles. Some of these, usually in wildly mutated form, ended up in the book; others were good stories, but didn't appeal to my hideous sense of the appropriate. In any event, many thanks to –

In England: Chris Peachment; Don Atyeo; Martyn Auty; Lesley Bryce; Gordon Burn; Graham Coster; Simon Garfield; Steve Grant; Peter Grimsdale; Richard Hammond; Andy Harries; Jude Harris; Jason Hartcup; Joanna Head; Michael Herr; Tony Heywood; Angus Mackinnon; William Maclean; David Pirie; Jennifer Potter; Lucretia Stewart and *Departures*.

In Los Angeles: Brad Auerbach, a great guide and an even greater friend; Glenn Auerbach, the brother from another planet; Marc Behm; Danny Heaps, whose knowledge of the freeway system was, incredibly, worse than my own; Jim Irwin, still looking for tasty outside waves; Jane Irwin, art expert and perfect lady; Victoria Irwin, who didn't know where the buses went; Mary-Ann, whose attitude was in need of adjustment; Big John McCrea, expert in Los Angeles history and emphatically no relation to the character of the same name in the book; Barker Price, may all his options be taken up by Universal; Bob Price, a fellow admirer of fat girls in Las Vegas; Eric Seder, who has at last asked enough women; Mio Yukovic, a fellow admirer of The Sweet. And: Grace Jones, David Lynch, John Milius, Jack Nicholson, Al Pacino, the late Lee Marvin, and the girl in the Scream club who told me 32 was 'awful old' to be a writer.

I owe a particular debt to Christopher Petit, Anne Billson, my publisher David Godwin and, most of all, to *Granta* editor Bill Buford who first suggested that the story of Barbara and Richard might be worth writing. All four put up with me long beyond the call of duty.

It goes without saying that the faults of the book belong to the above, and are not my own.

'Poor dope. He always wanted a pool.'
William Holden in Billy Wilder's *Sunset Boulevard*

'The intervals of lust were filled up with the basest amusements.'
Edward Gibbon, *Decline and Fall of the Roman Empire*

for Barbara, wherever you are

CONTENTS

PART
—1—

DIVING

I MET HER in a bar and knew I was in trouble. It was in a small fishing port on the south coast of Crete, early in the spring, and the bar was gloomy, almost deserted, its walls smeared with the bodies of crushed insects. She sat on a stool at the counter, laughing. She had large green eyes and slender, tanned arms. She was beautiful. She was also in a stupor, and gazed into a glass of ouzo. I introduced myself.

'Richard,' she said. 'Why aren't *you* drunk?'

Her name was Barbara. She was twenty-two and came from Buffalo in upstate New York and now lived in Los Angeles, waitressing and picking up modelling work whenever she could. During the summer of 1984 she and a friend took a stall on Venice Beach, selling shirts marked 'Los Angeles Olympics – Official Terrorist'. Then a real terrorist hijacked a bus, started running over people, and Barbara and her friend stopped selling the shirts. She said, 'I just kinda hang out. I might become an actress. Or the next Madonna.' She had thick, blonde hair and I thought she'd walked straight out of a surfing movie.

We met again the next day. It was sunny with a cool wind and we went to look at a ruined villa. A pair of stone lions stood guard. There were broken columns and limestone slabs. Barbara was unimpressed and sat on a bench, plunging herself deeper into her bomber jacket, tilting her face to the sun.

'Just a bunch of rocks,' she said.

'The book says Theseus might have stayed here.'

She popped her gum and thought for a moment. 'Guy with a ball of string in the maze, right?'

'That's right.' When we left she took the gum from her mouth and stuck it in the eye of one of the lions.

In the bar that night she told me she had a boyfriend called Patterson who rented a house in the hills above Hollywood and was trying to sell movie scripts. He wrote horror stories, she said, and his agent thought he might be able to land an episode in the new *Twilight Zone* series. It was late, and on the stereo Elton John sang, 'B-B-B-Benny and the Jets'.

'Don't worry,' said Barbara suddenly. 'Really.'

'Who's worrying?' I said.

'He's a nice guy,' she said, 'I can feel it,' and I began to suspect that Barbara wasn't talking to me. Her green eyes stared at a space between the tables in the middle of the bar. There was no one there. She smiled at the space, shaking her head. 'You saw that?' she said. 'But I was so drunk. It was hysterical. And when I poured the beer over the guy's head, I thought I was going to die. And did you see what the bozo did after that? Ohmigod, I can't believe you really saw that.' She nodded enthusiastically. 'Yeah, yeah, I'll be careful, I'm sure I can take care of everything.'

I was a little confused. She was quiet for a moment, then turned to me. 'What do you think of him?' she said.

'Who?'

'My father.'

'Your father?'

'He was here just now.'

'But there was no one.'

'Are you sure?'

'I'm sure.'

'Oh,' she said, and was silent. She said her father had died when she was seven. It had happened very suddenly but it was OK, she said, because he had been a great man and in any case he still came and spoke to her, told her what she was doing right, what she was doing wrong, gave her advice of all sorts. I gave her a furtive look. Did she believe this stuff? She did. Her delivery had an insane conviction. Her father had been a professor at Cornell, she said, a teacher of literature and philosophy, a 'totally brilliant guy'. She smiled and kissed me hard on the lips. I might not have been sure what was happening, but I liked it. I looked at her and saw: adventure.

I belonged to a generation raised on stories of glamour, stories of violence and excitement, stories of America. I was born in 1956 and brought up in Bradford, a soot-caked Victorian city, then capital of the north of England's wool industry. My father had been in the RAF during the Second World War and had since pursued various activities – farmer, undertaker, garage owner, rally driver – without notable success. He seemed often to be in trouble with the law, and loved cricket. Watching him imitate Len Hutton's square drive, stepping quickly down the lawn, bat flowing in an extravagant follow-through, was better than watching television. My mother was more realistic, a red-head, tiny and determined, used to living with uncertainty. This was just as well. My earliest memory, aged five, was of living in a big house that smelled of fresh paint and father coming home one night and announcing he had sold up. He said we were moving up the road, over the moor to Keighley, moving *that night*. My mother's reaction was calm. She packed glass and china in chests lined with tissue paper and crinkling silver foil, helped by my elder brother and sister. I was wrapped in a blanket and bundled into the large, square van hired by my father. I fell asleep, not waking until we were on our way. I pressed my face against the cool glass of the windscreen and heard my brother sing Eddie Cochran.

Step one, you find a girl to love
Step two, she falls in love with you
Step three, you kiss and hold her tightly
Yeah, that sure feels like heaven to me.

My brother collected rock-'n'-roll records and American horror comics, weird stories which he read out loud, like the one narrated by a six-year-old girl who shot her father and arranged for her mother to be executed for the crime. 'An ambulance wasn't what they needed. They needed a morgue wagon. In *our* state murderers die in the electric chair.'

'Morgue wagon,' I chuckled, not understanding the words.

'Yank rubbish,' said my father, thrusting the comics into the flames of the kitchen grate. Soon after that I began to collect the cards which came wrapped in wax paper with strips of pink, sweet bubble gum. A lurid series entitled 'The American Civil War' was my favourite. One card showed a grey-uniformed Confederate being bayoneted at Gettysburg. Scarlet blood fountained from his guts. Another showed 'The Rape of Georgia'. This posed questions. Such as: what was rape? and who was Georgia? Was she dark like my sister, or fair like Diana, the girl who sat in front of me at school and whose neck I had kissed during afternoon prayers?

Each Thursday I watched *The Saint* on TV. Roger Moore played a secret agent type who drove a white sports car. Suave, aloof, he treated women and adversaries with the same amused disdain. One night the programme was interrupted by a news-flash. My father was out, my mother in the kitchen, crouched over a pile of linen. Steam hissed from an iron and I told her: 'President Kennedy's dead.' My mother looked blank. Then she struck my face, the only time she ever hit me, and told me not to tell lies. My cheek burned. Nothing I'd ever said had prompted such a reaction from an adult. I asked, 'Who was President Kennedy?' and my mother must have realized I was telling the truth. She cried.

I grew older, learned about President Kennedy, saw *Dirty*

Harry, Bonnie and Clyde and a pair of rain-slicked thrillers from the 1940s in the same week at the Essoldo Cinema on Manningham Lane, went to college, almost became a lawyer, drifted into journalism, moved in with a woman called Jane who worked in television and loved cats, yet somehow never went to America, even though it had been there from the beginning, lined up for me, a mystery waiting to invade my life.

Then I met Barbara. I was twenty-seven, bored, and she was beautiful, restless, mad, like a prom queen who had cracked up. We spent a few hours on Crete, and then she went home. That, I suppose, should have been the end of it.

Back in London I stopped going to work and haunted the Underground, riding the loop on the Circle Line, exploring easterly offshoots of the Central. One weekend Jane and I drove out to Denver Lock in Norfolk. A river, two canals, and a series of water-filled ditches met there like spokes in a wheel. I climbed a bank and looked across the Fens. It was desolate: flat brown fields stitched together by seams of water, the pencil-thin figure of a parachutist drifting slowly from a grey sky. Behind, water boiled in the lock. That night we ate at a restaurant in Cambridge. The tablecloth was thin and frayed. Jane ordered chicken, I had lamb and poured the wine, a glass for her, one for myself, and watched her drink, slim hands cupping the glass as she lifted it to her mouth. She talked about her family, about the problems her father (amiable ex-army officer, taste for pink gin) was having with his knee joints, and about her sister, who was thinking of moving to Stoke. *To Stoke?* I half listened, drinking wine I didn't really want, and thought of Barbara. I thought of her gulping ouzo at the bar, chewing gum at the villa with the stone lions, telling me crazy stuff about *her* father. I knew I had to see her again.

'How's work?' said Jane. The question gave me a jolt. Had she found out I wasn't going to the office?

'Not bad,' I said.

'When are you going to change?'

'I'm sorry.'

'You don't seem to enjoy it any more. The work. You seem distracted.'

'Do I?' I said, and felt relieved. She didn't know.

We drove back to London in silence. The next day I called my brother, Todd. Sirens screamed in the background. I told him I'd met someone who had conversations with her father even though he died fifteen years ago. I told him I couldn't stop thinking about her. He told me I'd been with Jane for five years and was losing my marbles. I hung up, collected my passport and took the Tube to Heathrow. At Terminal Three I saw that a flight to Auckland, New Zealand, was leaving in two hours. It was a flight to Auckland, New Zealand, via Minneapolis, via Minneapolis *and* Los Angeles. I was behaving like a hysterical adolescent. But I was a hysterical adolescent with a credit card and there was a seat available.

I sat by a window. I was on the plane to California, on the 1a.m. from everything that was real, playing at adventure, taking a 7,000-mile trip on impulse and thinking: what an interesting movie I'm making. I remembered Auden's remark that any marriage, happy or unhappy, is infinitely more interesting than any romance, however passionate. I had something like a marriage at home. It was hard work. Auden, it seemed to me, didn't know shit.

The man next to me was bald and nervous. He clamped his teeth tight and muscles stood out from his thick, pale neck. After the plane had taken off he relaxed. He was Greek and a policeman, on his way to Los Angeles to make an arrest. He had a strange vision of America. There would be, he hoped, a picture of Marilyn Monroe at the airport.

'It must be an important case,' I said. 'They're sending you a long way.'

'The case? Yes, I suppose it's important,' he said.

The inflight movie was *Rocky 3*. Rocky clubbed it out against a huge black boxer with oak-tree arms and a Mohawk haircut. The bald man punched his fists in the air. 'Dead or alive,' he chuckled.

Hours later the plane began to descend. I looked out of the

window and there was Los Angeles, huge and sprawling, stretched out in the sun, an endless possibility. My heart was in my throat.

'You heard of Khrushchev?' said the bald man. 'Nikita S. Khrushchev? He used to be leader of Russia'

'I've heard of him.'

'He came to America in 1960. It was a famous trip. Lots of publicity, lots of photographs. He flew in to Los Angeles and he looked down, saw all the swimming pools, shining, gleaming in the sun. You know what he said?'

'No.'

'He said, "Now I know Communism has failed."'

The cab was blue and white, a Chevrolet. A sign hung from the mirror, saying 'Welcome to California. Adjust your Attitude'. I sank against the hot plastic seat, opened a window, let the warm air buffet my face. I didn't need the advice. I was an Englishman, in love with the idea of America. 'Check that,' said the driver as he negotiated a banked corner on the freeway. He pointed to a concrete building like a fortress, topped by battlements and adorned with sculptures of Babylonian priest kings. The building was coloured a violent pink.

'Disneyland?'

'Big tyre factory,' said the driver. 'I worked there. Two years.' He was lean, relaxed, long-haired. An ID card on the windscreen gave his name as Wen Shung, date of birth 12.15.55. I asked where he was from.

'Cambodia. I have lived in Los Angeles sixteen years. All my life,' he said. 'You been here before?'

'It's my first time.'

'American women are very strange,' he said. 'Each one thinks she is movie star.' He fiddled with the radio, spinning the dial until he found a station playing classical music, and asked if I liked Benjamin Britten. 'He is greatest modern composer. I was four years at music school. Now I compose,' he said, waving a sheaf of manuscript paper. 'My first violin sonata. This is my dream.'

He said, 'You meet American girl in Century City?'

'That's right.'

'She is strange?'

'In some ways,' I said. He grinned, pleased that I'd confirmed his theory. He said all American women liked to behave like Mata Hari. I said I hoped not.

I had arrived. At a nearby table two men were talking up a movie deal. One was tanned and relaxed, with a beard like Fidel Castro. The other had a desperate manner, purple lips and a terrible face. He looked as if he was unaccustomed to daylight, and in need of help urgently.

'Last weekend I saw Spielberg on the beach at Malibu,' said the man with purple lips. 'I've got a house there, you know, just something small, nothing much, nothing like your place. Anyway. Steven was there with his kid. Max. You know Max? Great kid. And Steven was doing this trick, holding his fingers like a rail and letting the baby swing on them. You see, a baby's grasp is so strong he'll never fall. Isn't that amazing? They got up to go and when they left there was a hollow in the sand. I went and sat in that hollow and thought, "What was going on in your mind, Steven? What was going on in your beautiful mind?"'

His bearded companion nodded. He was lighting a cigar the size of an Exocet. When it was ablaze he drew on it and billowed smoke into the face of the man with the purple lips. 'One thing the Cubans do real good,' he said. 'Boy, this is a stoker. Torpedo shaped. *Gangster style.*'

I was having trouble taking all this in. 'This place is too much,' I said, and it was. It was gaudy and faded and the colour of left-over mustard.

'Just a lot of men who want to party,' said Barbara.

'With you?'

'One guy pays me 500 bucks to swim naked in his pool. Wears these weird, red beach shorts while I do it and sings opera. He never touches me. He's a producer and his brain is gone. Pure ozone. Holly-*weird*.'

I was in shock. I was in Los Angeles and I had found Barbara. But she was wearing ears. She was also wearing five-inch turquoise stilettos and towered above me. Her breasts were supported by a corset of turquoise satin and a white pom-pom waggled on her backside: Bunny Barbara.

She kneeled beside me. 'You're crazy, you know that? Why didn't you tell me you were coming?' She pulled my head down and kissed me. My arm was around her and I felt the sweat between her shoulder blades.

'Have you worked here long?'

'Didn't I tell you about it?'

'I don't think so.'

'How did you find me?'

'I called the house. Someone said you were here. Was that Patterson?'

'Could be.'

'Are you pleased to see me?'

'What do you think?' she said.

I wasn't sure what I thought. Barbara didn't stop work until four, and her friend Lorraine had been invited to a water-sports party at a house in a place called Coldwater Canyon. She said, 'You and Lorraine'll get along great. She's from London, England.' Lorraine was the white bunny. She was togged out entirely in white and her hair had been soaked in peroxide. She looked like Diana Dors on mescalin. My mind was still racing: *a water-sports party?*

I'd always loved big, ostentatious American cars and Lorraine drove a beauty, a white Cadillac Eldorado, a convertible with montrous headlights and fins sharking from the rear. I clambered in and she said, 'We'll 'ave to make a detour. Oi've gotta pick up vese two geezers,' in a Cockney accent so exaggerated I almost laughed. *Come on*, I was about to say, and glanced at Barbara.

'Isn't Lorraine great?' she whispered.

'Absolutely.'

Lorraine drove erratically, saying 'I always get the brake and the gas mixed up,' and the Eldorado lurched and pitched and stuttered all the way to wherever it was we were going. Barbara sang along to Roxy Music on the radio and I fought off nausea in the back, wondering what she felt about my unannounced arrival. If she was beside herself with excitement, she was concealing it well.

We pulled up in front of a wood-framed bungalow, painted in vivid blue and with red shutters. Lorraine honked the horn. Nothing happened. She honked again. 'And it's drowning the sound of my tears,' crooned Barbara.

Lorraine lifted a cowboy-booted foot, kicked the horn, waited a few seconds and repeated the process. 'Where are they?' she shouted.

'Lighten up,' said Barbara.

'Jack! *HOO*-TER!' screamed Lorraine.

'They'll be here.'

'They're taking their bleeding time about it.'

Then the blue front door swept open and Jack and Hooter emerged, lumbering down the path, shouting LORR–AINE! and brandishing quart-size cans of shaving foam. A gob landed in my lap with a squelch.

'Will you just look at these guys,' said Barbara. I *was* looking. I couldn't help it. Jack and Hooter were wearing gorilla suits.

The house was high in a canyon, overlooking a neat garden with tennis court and swimming pool. The hosts were a minor movie star and her boyfriend, former kick-boxing champion of Denmark, now also an actor. She was tiny, blonde and improbably beautiful. He was just improbable: blond, bronzed and built like a skyscraper. Even his eyebrows were intensely muscular. She was in the shallow end of the pool with a margarita in one hand, trying to organize a game of water polo.

'C'mon Benny,' she was saying, 'you've got to play. Don't be such a dork.'

She looked around to enlist support and saw me. 'Tell Benny not to be such a dork. Get him to play. He was on the swim team at USC.'

I said I thought Benny should definitely play.

'*There!*' she said.

A triangular hulk of bronzed muscle stepped forward and jabbed me in the throat, hard, with a finger. 'Penis breath,' it said. This was Benny. He leaped into the pool and sank.

'Benny's bombed out of his brain,' said Barbara. 'He'll drown.'

I said, 'Are those the water sports?'

We walked to the tennis court where the Dane, legs crammed into red-and-white running shoes, calves bulging out of white socks, had stripped off the rest of his clothes and was taking on all-comers. 'Bring your money,' he shouted in his clipped accent. 'Bring all your money. One game. I give odds of five to one.'

The Dane lobbed up a ball and sent down a serve like a missile. Two challengers were blasted from the court then one of the gorillas ambled forward, swinging his arms and waving five twenty-dollar bills. He picked up a racket and scratched his head like King Kong. He examined a tennis ball as though it were an object from Mars. At last he was ready to play. The Dane took the game easily, penis bobbing in the cool, early evening air. The real win was the gorilla's, however, and afterwards he had a woman on either arm. He gave them proprietorial, simian hugs.

'Are you Jack or Hooter?' I asked.

'I think I'm Hooter but I'm not sure,' he said.

'You know,' Barbara whispered, 'people's characters really change once they get in a gorilla suit.'

I looked around. It was growing dark. Light shone from windows in the house. The Dane had pulled on red satin shorts. Fistfuls of dollar bills were stuffed down the waistband and he stood beneath a floodlit basketball hoop, saying 'I am Kareem, I am James Worthy, I am Kurt Rambis, who will play a game with me, one-on-one?' There were shouts from the pool. Lots of women, all tanned and beautiful, California girls even if they weren't girls from California, gathered round him. I felt tired.

I said to Barbara, 'Can't we go somewhere?'

She said that Lorraine wanted to go to the beach with Jack and Hooter. We could go with them. Didn't that sound neat?

Around midnight the Eldorado nosed along the ocean front, I'm not sure where, and we spilled on to the beach. Jack, or it might have been Hooter, ran headlong into the roaring, dark Pacific surf, beating his chest with one hand, cradling a bottle of tequila in the other, calling 'Guacamole, I want guacamole, tubs of. . . .' His voice cut off suddenly, and he disappeared.

'Where is he?' said Lorraine.

I stared at the ocean, saw only the white caps of the waves.

'HOO-TER!' shouted Lorraine.

'Wasn't it Jack?' said Barbara.

'Where *is* Jack?' said Lorraine.

'He could drown. The currents are real bad here,' said Barbara. 'Oh, Jesus.'

'I'm scared,' said Lorraine.

Infected by their panic, deranged with jet lag, I ran along the shore, shouting 'Jack! Hooter! Jack! Hooter!' and a hundred yards up the beach became airborne. I landed with a thump. Sand burned my cheek. I'd tripped over something: the gorilla, flat on his back, gazing at the sky, laughing.

'Just think about it man,' he said. 'This is it. This is where America ends. It's something else.'

I called to Barbara and Lorraine.

The waterlogged gorilla suit was so heavy we had to carry him back to the car.

'Are you Jack or Hooter?' said Lorraine.

'Jack,' mumbled the gorilla.

Then where, I wondered, was Hooter?

It was after three when they dropped me with my suitcase at the hotel, an imitation French château in beige concrete on Sunset Boulevard. Barbara told me it was here John Belushi died, strung out on booze and cocaine. I said I wasn't feeling too good myself.

'Aren't you coming in?' I asked.

'Come to the club tomorrow,' she said, and before I could protest a gorilla fist pulled the door shut and the Eldorado was off with a roar. I watched the tail-lights go down Sunset Boulevard, weaving: Lorraine was still having trouble with the brake and the gas.

The desk clerk was regimental gay: close-cropped hair, drooping moustache, lumberjack shirt with a name tag saying 'Hi. Je suis Gregory'. He looked me up and down with prim eyes and said, 'How has your day been, sir?'

I thought about this. I was soaked, exhausted, and my trousers were full of sand. I had failed to persuade Barbara to come to the hotel. My day had not been good. I asked if I could check in to the room where Belushi checked out. 'You have to book into that a month in advance,' he said, rattling a pencil against his teeth. 'Did you know that cocaine is the name of a men's store in Acapulco? *Strange.*' He sighed, and led me to a room on the third floor. From the window I saw a floodlit billboard, seventy feet high, advertising *Mad Max Beyond Thunderdome*. Mel Gibson looked at me with huge, brooding eyes.

I fell asleep with my clothes on and didn't wake until after midday. I showered, and waited for a cab outside a building that resembled a witch's castle and was in fact a bar called 'Carlos 'n' Charlie's'. A large sign advertised forthcoming appearances by 'SOMEONE DROWNED IN MY SWIMMING POOL'. What was *their* line? I wondered. Cars seemed to glide by in slow motion, obstructed by the thick, wobbling heat. My head buzzed and I was already sweating. I felt awful.

Thirty minutes later, a cab pulled up.

'Wreck?' said the driver with an unpleasant smile.

It was precisely how I felt. I thought it rude of him to comment. I said, 'What did you say?'

'Your car been in a wreck?'

'Oh,' I said. 'Now I understand. I don't drive.'

'You *don't* drive?'

'I never learned.'

'How long you been in LA?'

'A day.'

'You got money, pal?'

I asked if he would take a credit card and he whistled through cracked and discoloured teeth. 'Brother,' he said, 'and every time they saw up a woman I get the half that eats.'

The door of the Playboy Club was decorated with a bronze bunny head in the style of Giacometti. Inside, a squat, red-faced doorman chuckled and grinned. He wore an awful hairpiece that was like a pan scourer and a tight-fitting maroon suit through which he bulged and rippled. He stood at a counter where various Playboy items were on display: bunny watches, bunny airline bags, bunny bikini briefs, and a placard of Mel Torme commending a bunny lotion whose function was obscure.

'See that guy over there, going to the bar?' said the doorman, clutching my arm, unable to contain himself. 'Lotsa dark hair, walks like a cowboy?'

'I see him.'

'That's Joe Namath. Toughest quarterback I ever saw. Old Broadway Joe.'

This was of no interest to me. I told him I'd come to see Barbara. He looked angry. Perhaps he was appalled by my philistinism concerning Joe Namath. 'She ain't here yet,' he said.

'I'll wait.'

'Well, you'll have to buy a drink. That's the regulation.'

The bar was like a set for a Swinging London movie: mirrors and polished chrome cocktail shakers, high chairs with bucket seats and yellowing cushions, lamps in which red fluid made changing patterns. I ordered vodka and orange. This arrived in a glass decorated with the bunny logo. I gulped it down and asked for another.

The only other customer was the man who was supposed to be Joe Namath. He was about forty, swarthy and big, and hunched over a bowl of peanuts. He wore a lemon-coloured jacket. The material looked expensive, cashmere perhaps, or alpaca. 'You in the business?' he said in a growling voice.

'The business?'

'Movies.'

'No.'

He said I didn't drink like I was in the movies. No one who was in the movies drank any more. He regretted this. It cramped his style when he was around people who *were* in the movies. 'If you're not in the movies in this town,' he said, 'they don't think you're working. These guys give me a pain. 'Course, I made a coupla movies once. Machine guns and brutality, like *The Dirty Dozen*. Ever see that?'

'Robert Aldrich, Lee Marvin. Good film.'

'You got it,' he said. 'Now Lee, there was a man who knew how to drink. Got drunk with him one time down in TJ. It was Lee who warned me about English fruits. You get some guy carrying a cane, wearing a silk hat, he's got a pink hankie in his pocket and some great flower behind his ear and you watch your ass. That guy's a killer. He'll knock you down, piss in your eyes. You ever meet an English fruit like that?'

I said I never had. He found this strange. 'You *are* from England?' he said.

Before I could answer the barman put a phone in front of me. There was a call.

'Hi, hon,' said Barbara. She told me a modelling assignment had come up and she wouldn't be able to see me today. I said that was a shame. 'Lorraine's gonna take you to dinner,' she said. I said that was nice, thinking *oh shit*.

'Later, baby,' she said, and hung up.

The man who was supposed to be Joe Namath said, 'Female problem.'

'Something like that.'

'Fucking dames,' he said. 'Even when they do have gams the size of Cuban pineapples. Fucking dames.'

'Didn't you used to play football?'

'Who told you that?'

'The doorman.'

'Like I said, I'm an actor.'

'You're not Joe Namath.'

'Joe *Namath*. Guy's been jerking your chain.' He pushed away his empty glass, signalling for a refill and asked if, by any chance, I was one of those English fruits Lee Marvin had told him about.

The doorman was still by the gift counter, still smiling, brushing dirt from the sleeve of his jacket with plump fingers. 'She hasn't arrived yet,' he said, scowling.

'I know,' I said. 'The man at the bar said he wasn't Joe Namath.'

The doorman grinned: 'That Joe, he's such a kidder.'

It was lunchtime. Century City was full of Italian jackets, Gucci loafers and eyes sliding sideways towards each other, asking 'Do *you* drive a Porsche Targa?' I bought a copy of the *LA Times* and found a table at the Yum-Yum Diner. 'Minnie Mouse fondler jailed' said the headline on page seven.

> British visitor Julian Jones has been jailed for sexually assaulting Minnie Mouse in the Disneyland parade last week. Jones, 22, from Manchester, England, said, 'It was all a big misunderstanding. I'm not a pervert. I didn't think there would be a girl in the costume. I just assumed it was a male in there.' The victim of the crime was 18-year-old Loyola student Laura Morris. She had been working at Disneyland only three days. 'He definitely fondled me,' she said. 'This guy had his hands on my butt. He had his hands all over Minnie.' Jones received a three-month sentence and has also been banned for life from the Anaheim leisure complex.

I wondered what awful sexual despair could lead a man to assault Minnie Mouse. A waitress came for my order. She had hair like scrambled eggs and a tired, leathery face. I scanned the menu. The variety of choice was bewildering. I asked for something called 'The Entertainment Lawyer Special'. It seemed to be a ham sandwich.

'Supersalad?' she said.

'Yes, please,' I said.

'Supersalad?' she repeated, deadpan. I didn't understand the game.

'Yes, please,' I said, with a smile this time.

'*Supersalad*,' she said, raising her voice. She was getting angry now.

'No thanks, not today.'

'Listen up, fella. I don't have the time. Do-you-want-soup,' she said enunciating the words as if she were talking to a child of doubtful mental ability, 'or-salad?'

'I see,' I said, 'you mean do I want soup or . . .' and a nervous laugh escaped my lips.

That night I tried to call Barbara. Her answering machine played weird music with sliding guitars. I left a message, asking whether it might be possible, actually, for us to get together at some point. Lorraine knocked on the door of my room at eight. She wore a short black dress with zips all over. The words 'You'll be lucky' were stencilled where the filmy material hugged her thighs. White hair flew from her head at all angles. She'd been kissing an air-conditioner, and her boyfriend was in tow.

The boyfriend was Chuck. He was in A&R at Warner Bros. Chuck had freckles and staring eyes like chunks of broken sky. His trousers were baggy and made from parachute silk, tied at the ankle with gold ribbon, and he wore a T-shirt advertising a health-food store in Pasadena. 'Bliss for the Bowels', said the logo. Chuck and Lorraine were like walking billboards. I wondered whether I shouldn't get a message written on *my* clothing.

Chuck gave me a damp handshake. 'Did you *really* fly from London just to see Barbara?'

'Actually, I came to take home a swimming pool. I heard there were plenty round here, and cheap,' I said, and shuffled my feet.

Chuck behaved as though I hadn't spoken. He ignored my awkwardness, or hadn't noticed it. 'That's so amazing,' he said. 'I have this rule. It's called Chuck's Law of Geographic Desirability. Never, repeat, *never*, date a girl who lives more than twenty-seven minutes ride on the freeway. Lorraine's twenty-one and one half. Twenty-one and one half is reasonable. London is not. Am I right or am I right? Tell me. Lorraine, am I right, baby?'

'Right, Chuck.'

'And where is Barbara anyway? What is this beachwear commercial? Bikinis or one-piece?' said Chuck, and asked if I liked Chinese food.

Chuck drove an angular Japanese sports car, small and electric-blue with a bumper sticker: 'Pray for Me. I Drive Sunset'. He said, 'It's Sunset Boulevard, nine in the morning, the traffic's murder. They're scraping them up like strawberry jam. *Kiss that tarmac.*'

I was folded into the back, chin bouncing against my knees. From time to time I could see things: a palm tree, two motionless tourists staring at a floodlit mansion, a billboard which posed the question 'Is your number up?'

The car dipped into a tunnel. Lorraine explained to Chuck, 'Richard met Barbara when she was in Europe looking for her sister, Kimberley. The drooler. They finally got her put away, didn't they?'

This was news to me. I said, 'I never met the sister.'

'And didn't you two meet right after she had that thing with the Greek film director?'

The Greek film director? Barbara hadn't mentioned that.

'Wot woz his name? The Greek bloke. Barbara showed me a Polaroid. He even looked a bit like you.'

I tried to get my head round this. Lorraine thought I was a stand-in for a Greek film director? Chuck said, 'You met Patterson yet? The Tinseltown Raskolnikov?'

'Not yet.'

'I guess you will. And I'm sure you guys are gonna just love each other.'

'*Chuck,*' said Lorraine. 'You are awful.'

'What did Richard think? That Barbara would just walk out on Patterson and Patterson would just turn over and say, "Why don't you fuck me up there as well?"'

Chuck had a point. I wasn't sure what I'd thought. I hadn't really thought about it at all. We parked outside a cinema playing the new Eastwood movie and walked to the Chinese restaurant.

Through some cultural confusion the place had been given an Indian name, 'The Gunga Diner'. Illustrations from the Kama Sutra hung on the walls and the waiters were dressed in Nehru jackets to complete the Indian theme. They were blond and had Los Angeles tans. The nearest they'd been to India (or China) was a Satyajit Ray movie.

Lorraine ordered food, and Khyber Pass cocktails all round. These came in tall glasses and consisted of nine different types of spirit. They looked like those tubes of sand from the Isle of Wight which I used to get as a kid: each spirit was a different colour, each at its own level in the glass. 'Twelve of these and you really know you've 'ad a drink,' said Lorraine, inspecting her glass with satisfaction and draining it at a gulp. I followed suit. The taste was like sugar dissolved in petrol. It scorched my throat and I started coughing.

'You get used to the afterburn,' said Lorraine, ordering three more.

'You like Los Angeles?' said Chuck.

'I think so.'

'I *adore* Los Angeles. Think of any way to get rich, think of the most bizarre scam you can and somebody is doing it already. You want to start a hospital for kids' toys? You want to situate Cadillac wrecks on poles two hundred feet in the air? Some guy's already there. This town, it's creative.'

There was something Chuck liked even better about Los Angeles: relationships. It was so simple here, he said, you got the money, you got the glamour, you got the girl. 'It's so ... democratic,' he said, gazing at Lorraine as she downed another cocktail. 'Right, baby?'

'Right, Chuck.'

'I know, I know,' said Chuck. 'You're gonna say it's materialistic. But it's so simple it's beautiful. No bullshit. And if there's one thing I can't stand in this world, Richard, it's that one thing – bullshit. Right, baby?'

'Right, Chuck.'

After dinner it was back into Chuck's Japanese speedster for another hunchbacked ride, this time to the San Fernando Valley, to a club called FM Station where Chuck said Nip Drivers were playing. He was thinking of signing this band. He thought they could have a million hits. He said, 'And you should see the videos they've done. *Meet Me In St Louis* re-shot by Leni Riefenstahl. These are totally creative guys.'

The FM Station was tiny. Bodies were jammed against the stage and the sound system was a deafening fuzz of crackle and feedback. There were four of the Nip Drivers and they were on already, three skinheads and a girl playing bass who had silver hair and very unsteady legs. I thought she would topple off the stage at any moment. The singer waved a broken beer bottle, chanting 'The Holocaust is now, Hitler showed us how,' and the audience jumped up and down. Chuck was still at the door, in conference with someone he seemed to know well, a gaunt, dark-haired man in a big suit and with a gold swastika dangling from his ear. Lorraine asked me to dance and we headed for the clamour of music and eventful bodies. A fist came out of the crowd and knocked off my glasses. I didn't mind. The Khyber Pass cocktails were taking effect and I felt fine, ready for anything. Someone thumped me on the shoulder. It was Chuck, holding the wrecked remains of my glasses.

'These have been totalled,' he said. 'Just as well. Now you'll be able to get yourself some serious West Coast shades. Right, Richard?'

Right, Chuck.

I dreamt I was in a jungle. Undergrowth snapped beneath my feet and huge green leaves sweated with moisture. There were the shrieks of terrified animals and the smells of rotting vegetation. I met Barbara. She swam breast-stroke in a pool filled with black water. Was this a commercial for baby food? I asked. She came out of the water, standing close, so I felt the warmth of her body. She said, 'I just met the devil. He wears psychedelic shoes and runs a cut-price clothing store on Melrose.'

I woke up. The TV was on with no sound, showing *I Love Lucy*, the episode where Desi Arnez traps his head in the pineapple ice-bucket. I looked around. For a moment I didn't realize where I was. On the table by the bed was the wreckage of a steak sandwich which I must have ordered when I got back from the club the previous night and didn't remember eating. The bread had curled at the edges and looked dreadful. The phone was ringing. It was Jane.

She said, 'Tell me what you're doing in California. Tell me when you're coming back.'

'I'm not sure.'

'Which question does that answer?'

'Both, I suppose.'

'Is that all I get?'

'I met someone.'

'You mean you're fucking some girl?'

'Not exactly.'

'What do you mean? Exactly.'

'I'm not sure.'

I heard her draw breath. She said, 'I had to call the credit card company. They told me you'd bought a ticket to Los Angeles. I've been trying hotels for hours. You might have been dead for all I knew.'

'I think I am dead for all I know.'

'Richard, will you be serious?'

There was a silence.

'Is it fun being in love with someone else?'

On the TV Lucy had picked up a poker and was attempting to prise loose the ice-bucket.

'Fuck you, Richard. *Fuck you*,' she said.

I stared at the television.

'And the office called.'

'What did they want?'

'They said you hadn't been in for weeks. And if you don't come back straight away you're fired.'

I ate breakfast in the Café Hitchcock, a twenty-minute walk from the hotel in West Hollywood. I ordered coffee and The Rope-burger Surprise. This seemed to be a ham sandwich. A young woman sat with her companion in the next booth. She was slim, with dead white skin, straight black hair and features which were too precise. She looked like a mannequin and I wondered how she stayed so pale. 'Friend of mine knew this woman,' her companion was saying, 'she was just a secretary, something like that, and she wrote a script. She managed to get Michael Douglas to read it and he loved it and made it into a movie and she got a million dollars. First thing she did was to go out and buy a Lamborghini. Next thing she did was to kill herself in it on the Hollywood Freeway. Barbecued meat.'

The woman said nothing. She was immobile. Her eyes were dark grey and the shape of almonds, and they stared at a clock above the bar. A crazy thought went through my mind: that she might, actually, *be* a mannequin.

The companion was saying, 'That's what I call a *real* Los Angeles story.'

I went to the phone at the back and called Barbara. A man answered.

'Who is this?' he asked. The voice was husky with threat.

'Richard. Is Barbara around?'

'I'll see if she's still here.' I heard feet pad away, then shouting and glass breaking. I waited. Eventually she came to the phone.

'How's it going?' she said.

'What was all that noise?'

'Just some stuff going down in the kitchen.'

'I see.' I didn't. I told her that since I was here in Los Angeles it might be nice if we could – oh, I don't know – perhaps, well, *meet*.

'Sure,' said Barbara.

'We can?'

'I've got to go to the club and then on the assignment I was supposed to do yesterday. The guy's been jerking me around. Why don't you come along?' she said. She gave me an address in Marina del Rey.

'Where's Marina del Rey?'

'Get a cab,' she said and hung up.

I went back to my table and asked for the bill. The man with the pale woman was still trying to attract her attention. 'I know this stocky little guy,' he said. 'He's a friend of my father's, name of Amos, got the tattoo of a bulldog on his shoulder. He works over at Paramount and he used to be a navigator in B-52s. He told me they were out over Bakersfield one day – can you dig it? *Bakersfield* – and they dropped a bomb by mistake, a hydrogen bomb, 625 times as powerful as the one which trashed Hiroshima. And you know what? It didn't explode.' He smiled. He spread his arms wide in a gesture of disbelief. He shouted, 'Is California blessed or what?'

The pale woman continued to ignore him. I really was beginning to doubt whether she was alive. Perhaps the man shared this belief. His efforts became desperate. He knocked his forehead on the table. A salt-shaker went flying. He repeated the gesture. He knocked his forehead on the table over and over again.

At last the pale woman spoke. She said, 'I was down at the ocean last weekend and this guy said, "Why don't you go swimming?" I said, "I love the ocean but I wouldn't want to get involved." '

The photographer's name was Michael. He stood in front of a mirror, preening, rubbing his gums, teasing his hair, polishing his nails, admiring himself. He was in his forties with thick black hair to the shoulder. He wore faded jeans and his feet were tucked into snakeskin boots with four-inch heels. He was still very short. 'Look,' he said. 'I am not an asshole. So I changed the appointment. But I am not an asshole. OK?' He looked at us, seeking confirmation. Neither of us spoke. 'OK?' he repeated.

'OK,' said Barbara.

'OK what?'

'You're not an asshole.'

'Good.' He smiled, appeased, and stripped off his shirt to reveal bronzed torso and various gold chains and medallions in a forest of chest hair. 'Look at this,' he said, punching himself in the stomach. 'Rock solid. How old do you think I am? Guess. Go on.'

'About forty,' I said.

'Oh,' he said, and looked disappointed. He scampered around

busily, hoisting cameras over his shoulder, handing me a tripod, muttering words that sounded like 'going into turnaround with Universal', retrieving a bag of film from a sofa with the appearance and proportion of a baby whale.

The apartment was surgically neat: there were white rugs laid out at precise angles on a parquet floor, steel tables that looked like they should be used for autopsies, and gleaming racks of stereo equipment. A video screen covered one wall, while another was dominated by an oil portrait of Michael in tuxedo and blood-red bow tie, wearing a lopsided smile. In the picture he seemed absurdly young; was there another in the attic?

'OK,' said Michael, pulling on a blue T-shirt with cut-off sleeves, '*allons-y*, if we're going let's go,' and propelled Barbara towards the door.

A lift took us towards a subterranean garage. Michael whistled a few bars of a tune and said: 'You Barbara's agent?'

'Just a friend.'

'Along for the ride?'

I nodded.

'You look like a guy I knew in Paris. Ever been in Paris? City's full of dogshit. You know how many dogs there are in Paris?'

'I can't say I do.'

'Five hundred thousand. And each one of those little mothers has a squat on the sidewalk at least once a day. You can't get away from it. It's everywhere, the dogshit,' he said. 'And you know, the authorities have come up with six different methods. They have these six different methods for getting rid of the dogshit. *Six*. Mechanical scoops, stuff they spray on the sidewalk, Vietnamese boat people. And other methods. None of them work. The streets are like a combat zone.'

I was wondering where Michael obtained this curious information when the lift doors opened. The garage was echoing and harshly lit. Security cameras swivelled in every corner, tracking our movements. Michael unlocked the doors of a black Mercedes station wagon and we loaded equipment.

'I thought today we'd shoot in the desert.'

'In the *desert*?' said Barbara.

'Sure. Drive out towards Palm Springs and bingo. I've got an idea that'll knock you on the head.'

'You're the boss,' said Barbara.

'That's right,' said Michael. 'I *am* the boss.'

A snakeskin boot hit the accelerator with a thump and the Mercedes sped towards a spiralling ramp. Michael roared with glee, removing his hands from the steering wheel, saying 'Every day an adventure.' Barbara joined in the fun, laughing. I cowered on the rear seat.

On one of the freeways we came up behind an open-topped Volvo truck containing a billboard of Sigourney Weaver, wearing taut grey overalls ripped all over. She had a machine gun in her hands and she loomed over the Mercedes, held by ropes, rocking gently in the air-currents. Michael wound down a window: 'Hey, baby, you've got a beautiful ass.'

'What movie's that for?' I said.

'Some action picture. Stallone with tits. She can do better. You know Sigourney?'

'No.'

'She's into the I-Ching,' he said. 'She's got this hot deal with Fox right now.' The word 'deal' seemed to excite him. He became expansive. He talked about the movie stars he knew. He talked about his own plans. He was on the verge of a development deal with Paramount, was getting ready to pitch a story to Irwin Yablans at Empire, had two concepts over with Lorimar, a project that was about to 'go' at New World, and then there was a woman who had Spielberg's ear at Amblin' and was really hot for an idea he'd come up with for a children's science-fiction musical adventure. 'Imagine *Goonies* plus *South Pacific*. Wouldn't that be beautiful?'

'I never much liked *South Pacific*,' I said.

Michael frowned. He paused, breathing heavily. 'I think the point to remember here is that we shouldn't get bogged down in specific cases. This is not just an idea. This is a *groundbreaking* idea.'

'If it comes together, remember me,' said Barbara.

'Count on it, sweet thing. You stick to me, you'll get lucky,' said Michael and patted her thigh. His fingers were heavy with jewels and gold. 'What do you do in real life, Richard?'

'I'm a journalist,' I said, without thinking, and remembered the conversation with Jane. I was about to be fired. What would that make me? I looked out of the window. We were in a valley. Slopes rose steeply on either side, covered with trees. There was fruit on the trees: oranges. London seemed far away.

'What sort of stuff do you write?'

'Profiles, features, the usual things.'

'You know what would be a great subject for a story?'

'What's that?'

'Me.'

'I see,' I said. 'You?'

'Me.' I said nothing until finally Michael told the story of his life. He was forty-eight and had been married four times, each marriage more expensive than the last. He had been born in Czechoslovakia and his parents came to America in 1939, after escaping through France and England. He said that when Hitler invaded Czechoslovakia *Variety* reported the event by noting this would mean a drop in foreign film earnings of one and one-half per cent. 'Believe it,' said Michael. '*Variety* always gets the important facts.' He went to college in Philadelphia and came west in the 1950s. One of his wives left him for a movie producer, one was killed by a hit-and-run driver, another was now a famous actress. 'I never look back. The future is the excitement, a never-ending road, full of surprises,' he said, and it sounded like a well-practised line.

'We'll get lunch here,' said Michael, guiding the Mercedes through an arch formed by the legs of a dinosaur. The dinosaur was green, made from shaped fibreglass and must have been over 150 feet tall. A sign on its chest said: 'Welcome to Daddy Sugar's truck stop. I am Arnold, Southern California's biggest lifesize brontosaurus'.

A country and western show was advertised on the door of

Daddy Sugar's. Inside, fans whopped the air. We ordered and Michael went to play a video game. He hunched over the machine, fingers stabbing the controls.

'Barbara,' I said. 'I had this great idea. How would it be if I came and lived out here for a while? In Los Angeles. I thought it might be worth a shot.'

She said, 'Why?'

I mentioned that it would be possible, perhaps, for us to spend some time together.

'What about your job in London?'

'I think I'm going to lose it.'

'Because you came here?'

I shrugged.

'How come you're like this, Richard?'

I thought about this. How could I explain to her that I had lost my bearings, that I had come to California on an unstoppable impulse, and that a minute with her turned my brain to pulp? I remembered a conversation I'd had with a philosophy tutor when I was a student. He was stout, bald and bullet-headed, a little like Erich von Stroheim. He made controversial TV appearances in which, though himself a Christian, he denied that Christ was literally the Son of God; apparently it was a metaphor. He asked how my classes were going, I told him I was having trouble with ethics. 'My dear boy,' he said with a donnish chuckle, flicking a speck from his gown, 'I can only trust you mean in the theoretical and not the practical sense.'

I said to Barbara, 'I have trouble with ethical decisions.'

She said, 'You *are* crazy.'

Michael left the video machine. There was a woman, alone, twirling strands of blonde hair, and he slid in next to her, saying 'Hi. My name's Michael. I'm a photographer and I'd be real interested in taking your picture sometime soon.'

The woman was blousy and maternal. She twirled another strand. She said, 'You're putting me on?'

Michael gave her a smile of devastating sincerity. 'Are you crazy? Why would I do that? You have the most beautiful mouth I've ever seen.'

'You really think so?'

'Of course.'

'Really?'

'You *know* I think so.'

'I had a silicon injection in my lower lip. To make it swell, you know? I wanted to look like Ava Gardner.'

'And you do,' said Michael. 'You really do.' He asked for her phone number.

Michael came back to the table. He said, 'Let me tell you something, Richard. If enough women aren't saying no, you're not asking enough women.'

We drove on. The landscape became cracked, bleached, wild. We passed a military airfield and a graveyard for wrecked cars. 'Welcome poor boys' was sprayed in white on a corrugated iron fence. The car's air-conditioner hummed at full tilt and distant mountains were barely visible through the heat-haze. We turned off the highway and onto a rock-strewn track. '*Nous sommes arrivés*,' said Michael. 'This is the idea. The swimwear range is called "Madonna", right, and I'm going to shoot Barbara next to *that*.' He pointed. About fifty yards away in the desert there was a statue of Christ, wearing white robes, hands spread wide in a gesture of supplication. 'Is that a boss idea or what?'

I was about to say it came into the 'or what' category when Barbara said 'Genius', and opened the door. A rush of hot air took my breath away.

Michael set up his camera in the shade of a tree with twisted branches and leaves like bayonets. I sweated. The lack of noise was eerie. Sky, rocks and sand melted into the same colour, a thin, washed-out blue. Dragonflies hovered and a silver jet boomed overhead, cracking the silence.

Barbara turned on the radio and climbed into the back of the car. She started to undress. 'How do you want this?' she said.

'You're gonna do it like you're making out.'

'Making out?'

'Yeah. Like you think he's pretty cool, like you really, really, really want to fuck this Jesus guy.'

Barbara stood in front of the Christ, she pressed her breasts against His waist and thrust a knee towards His crotch, she rested her head on the entreating palm of one of His hands and kicked a gold-spangled stiletto toward the other. 'That's nice,' said Michael, crouched over a Hasselblad. Sweat dribbled on his chin. 'That's nice. But let's have some more. Do it, do it for me.'

Barbara moistened her lips slowly with her tongue, as if preparing to receive communion. She embraced the Christ. She caressed Him, moving her pelvis against His thigh with a slow, grinding motion. Michael called, 'Beautiful, beautiful, some guys have all the luck.' She crushed her mouth against the Christ's hip, leaving red lipstick stains like stigmata. Michael murmured, 'Oh, baby,' and sent me to the car for more film.

I found some boxes in the boot of the Mercedes and brought them back. Michael was now shouting, 'Cream, baby, cream all over Jesus for me.' He snapped a roll of film into the camera, and asked me to bring him a lens cap.

'Where is it?' I said.

'Don't bother me now,' said Michael. 'In the front somewhere.' I trudged back to the car, reflecting that running errands for a five-foot-nothing photographer who was encouraging a six-foot-something bunny girl to simulate orgasm with a religious relic had not been quite what I had in mind when I flew to Los Angeles.

Michael said, 'That's got it. It's a wrap. As my friend Bobby de Niro would say, "Finito".'

'You don't need the lens cap?'

'Lens cap? Who said anything about a lens cap?' He unscrewed the camera from the tripod. 'Lend a hand here, will you, Richard?'

I found the camera case, gave it to him, and picked up empty film boxes from the sand.

'You know Robert de Niro?'

'We went bowling together. Me and Bobby,' he said, holding up a hand with the first two fingers locked together, 'like *that*. 'Course, I don't see him as much as I did. He's become what they call a recluse. But we used to hang out a lot when he was making that movie, the one about the priest.'

'*True Confessions.*'

'That's the one. One of those movies didn't have any women in it. That's gotta be a mistake. That's what a movie is all about. Find a beautiful woman and point a camera at her.'

I was retrieving a lens filter from the sand when I saw something move. It slid beneath a clump of tumbleweed with an angry rattle.

'Snakes,' I squealed.

'Diamond-back. Usually they come much bigger.'

'Poisonous?'

'Oh yeah,' said Michael. 'But that one only bites when it's good and mad.'

I'd seen it; it had seemed good and mad to me.

'The Indians thought it was bad luck to kill them. They kept them in cages, used the venom as a sexual stimulant,' Michael informed me, his face twisting into an obscene leer. 'Keeps the lollipop hard.'

Barbara had changed again, back into jeans and a T-shirt. She wiped sweat from her face with a towel and asked what the fuss was about.

'I saw a snake. A huge bloody snake.'

'This was some idea of yours, Michael,' she said.

'My speciality.'

'Let's go, this place is giving me the creeps,' I said. Another jet went past with a boom.

'Sure,' said Michael. 'But first I thought Barbara might like to suck my penis.'

'You thought what?'

Michael looked at me as though I was trying his patience. 'You heard me. One, Barbara. Two, laughing equipment. Three, round my lollipop.' He counted off the points on his hand. 'Seems fair, and I won't be needing the snakes' venom.'

'You're out of your mind.'

'Don't say that. It doesn't really worry you, does it, Richard?'

'You're out of your bloody, fucking mind.'

'*Don't* say that.'

Barbara watched with an amused smile. 'He's not out of his mind, just an asshole,' she said.

'Don't you start.'

'You're an asshole, Michael.'

'I am not an asshole.'

'A-S-S-H-O-L-E,' she spelled.

Michael sighed and shielded his eyes against the glare. On the radio Patsy Cline sang, 'I love you honey, I love your money, I love your *auto*-mobile.' He looked at me. He looked at Barbara. He said, 'Fine. That's fine. I'll get back into the car and leave you both to the sun. And the snakes.'

I moved towards him. 'You jerk.'

He held up a warning finger. 'Don't mess with me. I'll fuck you mister, *and* the horse you rode in on.'

My mind screened possible scenarios. I imagined stepping forward, dropping my shoulder, swinging my fist and knocking Michael off his feet, being greeted by Barbara as a hero. That one wasn't bad. Then I remembered the fights I'd been in, usually lasting about five seconds and ending with me on the floor, clutching my groin. So, a rewrite: me swinging as planned, but Michael bobbing away, grinning as he crunched a pointy snakeskin boot into my balls and moved in for the kill, only to find Barbara swinging back her foot and letting him have it in the stomach. Air would explode from his stomach with a *whoosh* and he would fall to his knees. His expression would be bemused. Barbara would then deliver a chop to his head and survey the remains, pronouncing 'Out cold.' Long-legged Barbara, un-expectedly revealing herself to be a kung-fu expert, would come to the rescue. I drew back my fist.

'Stop it, you two,' said Barbara, pushing between us. 'Hold it there.'

Michael was laughing. 'Tell me, Barbara,' he said. 'Who does your friend think he is? John Wayne at Iwo Jima? Or some other movie idol?' He patted me on the cheek. 'England wants to be a hero. Never mind. Maybe he'll get the chance. But not today.' He announced that he was going back to LA. England was not getting a ride, he said, because England had been so aggressive. Barbara could do what she wanted. She could go back with him, or stay with Lawrence of Arabia in the desert. It was up to her.

'Fuck off, Michael,' she said.

He shrugged. I shuffled my feet on the hot, coarse sand. He stashed equipment in the back of the car and drove away. 'Asswipe,' she shouted. She said Michael was a second-class photographer and a first-rate jerk, a game player who always wanted to feel in control. Who needs that macho shit? she asked.

We were stranded. I didn't mind. The situation had potential. Barbara said we should walk back to the main road and hitch a lift. That wasn't what I had in mind. I suggested we could perhaps take off our clothes and screw right there in the desert. Jesus could watch. She said, 'If the snakes didn't get us, the scorpions would. Besides, I hate to fuck out of doors. It does something totally gross to the pores of my skin.'

She picked up a blue-and-gold bag with 'Los Angeles Rams' on the side and headed off down the rock-strewn track, telling me Michael had done something like this before, leaving her stranded outside Las Vegas. She'd had to hotwire a car. 'It was easy,' she said. 'Mom made my sister and me take a lesson.'

In hotwiring a car?

'She's a very far-sighted woman,' she said.

'Did she remarry? After your father died?'

'Yeah.'

'What's your stepfather like?'

'Mom's husband? He's a professional weight-lifter.'

We climbed a dusty path to the highway. The heat left me breathless. A stretched Lincoln limousine with smoked windows went past on the boiling tarmac, then four teenagers in a pick-up, shouting and hurling beer cans. A truck lunged and swayed through a mirage, and stopped. The driver was fat and wore greasy blue overalls. 'Strange place to be hitching a ride,' he said, and Barbara informed him I was from England. That seemed to explain it. 'Never met no one from there didn't need a saliva test,' he said. We were passing through a town called Riverside when we passed the Mercedes which moved slowly on the inside lane. Michael stared in front of him, grasping the steering wheel so hard, his knuckles were white. A black swimsuit was wrapped samurai-style round his head and he had a hunting knife clutched between his teeth. Barbara and I looked at each other, and laughed. I asked her to come back with me to the hotel.

She said, 'Why not?'

Gregory the desk clerk was in the hotel lobby with a group of Japanese tourists. There were about forty of them and they brandished cameras. 'This,' said Gregory as he stood beneath an iron chandelier, 'is the precise spot where Paul Newman met Joanne Woodward in 1957.' Barbara and I made for the lift.

In the room she looked out of the window. She said she had seen *Mad Max The Road Warrior* five times and she thought Mel Gibson was just the best. I placed my hands on her waist and kissed the back of her neck. She turned, pressing her lips against mine, running slender fingers down my arm. We undressed and lay on the bed. Her nipples were like peach-stones. My tongue explored a route down her body, past breasts, across belly and thigh to salty cunt. We fucked. I was lost to her reaction, lost to the honking traffic sounds that drifted up from Sunset, lost to everything. I couldn't believe this was happening. A fantasy had sprung to life. I was, actually, *in a movie*. Afterwards Barbara said (as I remember it) 'That was so nice' and I lay unable to sleep, with her beside me, breathing regularly, head resting on the crook of her arm. I watched the rhythmic rise and fall of her shoulder. It had happened. I had made it happen.

I couldn't keep still. I got up to go to the bathroom. Barbara's bag was on the chair. I picked it up. The bathroom light shone bright off the tile floor, straining my eyes. I opened the bag. Here was: comb, lipstick, eye-liner, underwear (it was clean), California driver's licence, a crinkled black-and-white of a couple in their late twenties on a lake in a small boat (parents?), a paperback titled *Rich Is Better* and a plastic bag from Neiman-Marcus. Inside this bag was Barbara's Bunny costume. I looked in the mirror, thinking about Jane back in London, about Michael in the desert, about Barbara asleep in the bed a few feet away. My face was tired and drawn.

I had to stretch the band to make the velvet ears fit. I pulled on the tights, which were elastic, and then the corset, which was snug across the chest. The green stilettos pinched less than I would have expected. I hadn't realized Barbara had such big feet.

I went back into the bedroom and stood at the foot of the bed, watching as she stirred slightly in her sleep. Outside a police siren went *whoo-whoo-whoo*. I fingered the pom-pom on my arse. I was in Los Angeles, I was transformed, I had finally arrived: Bunny Richard.

PART
—2—

COMING TOGETHER

'I LOOK LIKE like Cary Grant,' said David S. Takowsky, 'but Jewish.' Takowsky was a big Hollywood agent. Barbara had got me his phone number. 'Patterson thinks he's a real powerful man,' Barbara had said. 'Patterson thinks he can be real useful to you.' I'd said, '*Patterson thinks* . . .' and she'd just said, 'Yeah, he knows about these things, he's cool, he's thinking of your interests.'

Takowsky and I met for breakfast in the mall at Brentwood. By 10 a.m. the heat was building and on San Vicente the pink-flowering coral trees were motionless. I took a table outside Dutch's Deli and ordered coffee. I'd been waiting for a few minutes when a man strode through the mall, suave and tanned and tall, face creased in a confident smile, wearing an immaculate grey silk suit and a blue silk tie. His nose was sharp and beaky. It was Takowsky. He looked like Cary Grant, but Jewish.

He shook my hand, sat, and stood immediately, waving to someone across the mall, a woman in a white hat outside the book store. 'Catch you later, Legs,' he called. His accent was cultured, his entire demeanour suggesting *smooth*.

'That was Legs,' he explained. He smiled, I smiled: *Legs*. 'So you think you might be able to write movies?'

'That's the idea,' I said, and pushed towards him a copy of a script called 'Oozy Suicide' which I'd written with a friend in London. 'Oozy Suicide' was a girl-buddy horror story. There was lots of splatter and gore and sex. We sold it to an English producer with an Elvis Presley quiff and a face that hideously resembled a rodent. He hired an American director who told us: 'I know what you boys are up to. I've got *your* number. You've written a goddam lesbian art movie.' He told us he had hired another writer. We were off the picture. Two months later he got in touch again. This time he told us: 'Goddam new writer. He's putting in all these truly awful lines, just to sabotage *my project*.' We were back on the picture. Another month after that, one of the backers pulled out, removing his investment to a Bermuda tax shelter. The film was never made. Thus: my experience in the screen trade. I told Takowsky nothing. It seemed a shrewd move.

Takowsky was saying, 'I don't have to tell you how tough it is to break into screenwriting. The trouble with Los Angeles is that everyone's got the best story in the world. Not only that, everyone wants to be Larry Kasdan, everyone wants to be John Hughes. Even my manicurist has written three screenplays. Now *you've* got an angle.'

'I do?' This sounded encouraging.

'Your angle is that you're English. Unfortunately,' he continued, smiling, 'the main virtue of that particular angle is being English in England. Like Robert Bolt. Or David Lean. Out here you're just another hustler, with a cute accent.'

A waitress arrived and poured coffee. Takowsky gave her that smile. He said, 'However, I might be able to work with you so long as you understand that what counts for culture in this industry is something which the kids can dig. Something high concept.'

'High concept?'

'High concept.' He explained about high concept. It was

something which involved sex, or Sting, or the defiance of authority, or the destruction of valuable property on an absolutely massive scale, and preferably all four.

'Sounds like a cinch,' I said.

'I'll read your script,' he said, viewing the title page with obvious suspicion. 'Give me a call when you get a clue about some ideas. Perhaps we'll take a meeting. And remember . . .'

'High concept,' I said.

The woman from Garland Realty was small and trim, with curling blonde hair and high heels beneath her Calvin Klein jeans. She had a squint and a tiny dab of lipstick on her eye tooth. Her name was Judy. All the women at Garland Realty were called Judy, she said, it avoided confusion. She pulled up outside a blue concrete prefab on Venice Boulevard, about half a mile west of Culver City. She said, 'This is the cheapest apartment we have right now. A real sweet deal at $700 a month.'

An abandoned barbecue leaned drunkenly against the front door, rusting. I pushed it aside and Judy reached into her black leather shoulder bag for the keys. Inside, the living room was low, dark and bilious, carpeted with frayed matting and with a kitchen area and red formica breakfast bar at one end. Posters on the wall depicted Sylvester Stallone: with boxing gloves and bloody cheek, with pick-axe handle and donkey jacket, with mirrored sunglasses and matchstick gripped between angry teeth.

'Who lived here before?'

'A fan, I guess. Me, I was never really into those boxing movies. *Flashdance* was more of a learning experience.'

'Where's the bedroom?'

'This is it,' she said, jabbing a stiletto fingernail in the direction of a leatherette sofa the colour of tomato ketchup, 'it pulls down.' I tugged a handle at the bottom of the sofa and bounced on the squeaking mattress.

'What about the bathroom?'

'Through here.' She set off down a gloomy corridor. I followed her clicking heels.

The bathroom was black: black tile, black linoleum, black sink and bath. A mirrored black cabinet contained a rust-spotted razor and a bottle of Pepto-Bismol so ancient that the pink fluid was now dried up, cracked and cratered, with mould growing up the side.

'Nice bathroom,' I said.

Judy wasn't paying attention. She was flushing the toilet. She was saying, 'Ohmigod, I don't think I can handle this, that's just totally awful, I swear I think I'm going to barf.'

'What's the matter?'

She pointed. I looked into the toilet. I saw the corpse of an iguana, about nine inches long, with a scruff of spines around the neck. The corpse rose like a nightmare and for a moment it seemed certain the water would overflow, then the level began to sink and the corpse rotated slowly, tugged by currents. I suggested that we could remove the iguana and bring the old barbecue into action. Judy pressed a handkerchief to her lips. In these circumstances, she said, she was prepared to make a deal, $600 a month. That was her best offer.

'You don't have anything better?'

'Not at this price.'

I looked at my watch. I had to get back to Hollywood. Barbara was meeting me for lunch. I hadn't seen her for a few days. She'd been busy.

'I'll take it.'

She said, 'You will?' She said she needed a reference from my Los Angeles employer. I told her I had recently moved from London. She said my previous London employer would do just as well. This would have been fine except that a telegram had arrived at the hotel the previous week. WHYNONEWS, it had asked, CALL OFFICE SOONEST OTHERWISE NO ALTERNATIVE BUT TO TERMINATE CONTRACT STOP. Barbara had stood beside me as I replied: FUCK CONTRACT STOP YOUR MAGAZINE LACKING FUN HUMOUR STYLE FACT HUMAN INTEREST STOP MORE BUNNIES HERE STOP AND SUN STOP ANYWAY IM STAYING STOP.

'The reference could be a problem,' I said. 'I can always find another place.'

Judy looked around the apartment. 'I guess we can make an exception,' she said. 'In this one case.'

Barbara collected me at the hotel. She was late. Her car was a red Mustang, dented all over. She drove fast and as if distracted, talking, applying lipstick, switching stations on the radio, brushing hair from her face when the wind whipped it across. We barrelled up Sunset, past hot-dog stands and palm trees with tops like spider plants. Barbara drummed long, scarlet nails against the steering wheel. She hit the gas and the Mustang surged through a red light at Fairfax. 'That should get it,' she said.

A man wolf-whistled from the side of the road. 'You're *beautiful*, baby!' he called. 'Sit on my face.'

Barbara said she'd been talking with her father again. They'd had a long chat. He'd told her not to worry about Patterson and me. Everything would work itself out. It was a matter of the psychology of the emotions. I moved over and slid an arm across her shoulders. I told her I thought everything had worked itself out already: last week at the hotel. Barbara chewed at a nail. She said she wasn't going to rush into anything. 'I've known Patterson since I was fourteen years old,' she said. 'What do you expect?'

I remembered the previous November. My brother Todd had called from Beirut. He was working there for Reuters. He had been kidnapped and held hostage. The kidnappers were teenagers who brandished AK47s and walked stiffly with pistols thrust down the waistbands of their Levis. They snatched him from a restaurant in the Muslim sector, bundled him into the back of a Mercedes and drove across the city, firing shots into the air as they sped through checkpoints. One of them pressed a gun barrel to his temple and assured him he would find his brains in his lap if he moved a muscle. Another asked him if he liked the films of Clint Eastwood. They robbed him, then released him. Todd wanted to hear all about my life. He asked me to describe the taste of a pint of Bass.

I looked at Barbara. I expected my old life to be swept away. I expected passion and excitement and a movie to become real.

I asked, 'Where are we going for lunch?'

She said, 'My place.'

We were stopped in a jam outside the Sunset Grill. A man in a blue Chrysler wound down his window and asked for Barbara's phone number. Barbara ignored him.

I said, 'With Patterson?'

'He'll be there, I guess.' I told her I hadn't expected *that*.

Patterson sat in front of the TV watching a football game, empty beer cans scattered at his feet. He said nothing when Barbara and I arrived. He said nothing when Barbara said who I was and that I'd come for lunch. He was thin and bearded.

'He's so intense,' said Barbara.

She led me to an open window and onto a concrete balcony. Below, there were gum trees and a steep hill winding down to Sunset where traffic moved slowly. Hot rubber and exhaust fumes mingled with the smell of rosemary. 'Why do guys get so wound up about sport?' she said, looking at Patterson. She explained he was watching a college game between the UCLA Bruins and their rivals USC. Patterson had a large bet on UCLA.

'How large?'

'About $5,000.'

'Does he always bet such a lot?'

'Whatever he's got. He likes to gamble.'

'You don't say.'

Patterson stared at the TV with furious concentration, willing his team to victory, shouting, 'Go, Bruins, *go!*' Every time the UCLA quarterback completed a pass he slammed a fist into his palm and whooped. At the two-minute-warning he was beaming. UCLA had the ball, they were five points ahead, they had only to run down the clock and they were on clover. But USC came late with a destructive surge, forcing a fumble and crashing upfield for a touchdown in the last seconds.

Patterson said nothing. He gazed at the screen in disbelief, his eyes opening wide. Then he shrieked, picked up a Coors can and hurled it at the TV. The can hit and bounced away, leaving beery dribbles across the screen. Patterson slumped down the sofa, head in hands, and began to cry.

'Poor baby,' said Barbara.

'My God,' he said. 'I feel as though my parents died.'

'*Poor* baby.'

I helped Barbara make a salad and hamburgers. I chopped onions and said: 'I remember when United lost to Arsenal in the 1979 Cup Final. United were losing, 2–1, then we equalized in the last minute. Sammy McIlroy got the goal. I couldn't believe it. I went crazy. Arsenal kicked off and Brady, this great player, an Irishman, the only one on the pitch who kept his head, sent a beautiful long pass to Rix on the left. Rix looked like Harpo Marx. He humped it into the penalty area and Allan Sunderland scored with the last kick of the game. United lost. I was devastated for weeks.'

'Barbara. What's this man talking about?' said Patterson, his eyes cold and serious.

'Yes, Richard. What *are* you talking about?' said Barbara.

'I was just saying, trying to explain to Patterson. I know how he feels.'

Patterson scowled, and fingered the bread knife.

Barbara said, 'You know what happened at the club yesterday? Kim, she's the red bunny, the one who lives in that cute house by the canal in Venice, she got served with divorce papers. And she never even dates guys. Isn't that a blast? Turns out some friend of hers from high school married this bozo using her name, then ran away with his car and plastic and money. That's why these guys came looking for her.'

'I was in England one time,' said Patterson, 'and everyone spoke the whole time about *going to the loo*.'

'This happened in Big Springs, Wyoming. Wouldn't that make a great movie?' said Barbara.

'Why is that?' said Patterson. 'You guys obsessed with your own assholes or something? Like faggots.'

I bit down on my hamburger, and Barbara offered Patterson the salad. He looked glum. She asked how his new script was going. This cheered him up. He said it was going well: he had the first act, he had the characters, now he just needed the plot. He wanted it to be something really scary, like *Alien*, except with cats instead of a monster from outer space. He even had a title: 'Apocalypse Miaow'.

'Genius,' said Barbara.

'And this morning I got this other great idea,' he said. He gave me a strange look. 'Want to hear about it?'

'Why not?'

'It's for a story about caving. I used to do a lot back east, with my dad. You ever done that?'

'Never.'

'It's a great sport, real scary. The story's about a guy, he's going caving one weekend with his wife and his best friend and these two are having a love affair. Like, they're fucking each other.'

Patterson asked how I liked it so far. I glanced at Barbara, who smeared peanut butter on a slice of bread. My throat was dry. I said I thought the idea was interesting, strong. Patterson grinned. He said it got better. He described how the three characters are crawling through a narrow tunnel, with the wife and lover a little way ahead. Patterson moved his hands to indicate the weird shadows thrown against the walls by the lamps on their helmets. He did effects of water dripping on their faces: *plip, plop, plip.* He imitated the woman's sexy, husky voice as she told the lover of her conviction that the husband had guessed about the affair. Patterson generally got into the spirit of the thing. He said, 'They come to the end of the tunnel and then the camera pulls away and we see that they've come to the edge of nothing. The tunnel comes out in the middle of a cliff. Below, there's just this terrifying drop. The husband says, "We can't go back. We're just gonna have to go down. You two first. On separate ropes."'

At this point the lover should begin to get suspicious. But this man's brains are located in his penis. He's so stupid, Patterson noted, so *dumb* that he just eases himself over the edge and starts moving down, just asking for it. He's climbed down some twenty feet, and the woman is above him, watching and then his rope is cut, suddenly, and he's gone, *boom*, spinning into space.

Patterson finished his hamburger, pushing the remains of the bun between his teeth and chewing with satisfaction. He continued with the story. The lover's scream, he informed me, would be like nothing I'd ever heard. And the wife is crying now. She is hysterical, begging for mercy, her nails bleeding as they tear at the edge of a crack she's found in the cliff. The camera shows the husband's face and the audience understands that he knows everything. Moreover, he is gaining sadistic pleasure from his control of the situation. He reaches into his waterproof and pulls out the biggest hunting knife in the history of the world. It gleams. It could slice a man at twenty paces. With it the husband saws through the second rope, the one holding his wife.

Patterson said, 'Then he just walks away. Laughing. He knows the bitch can hang on for thirty seconds. A minute, tops. And then she's gonna fall and die, just like her lover. The last thing the camera shows is the fear on her face, and the end credits roll.'

Barbara's head was lowered and she slid a wedge of tomato through a pool of olive oil on her plate. Patterson sipped beer and seemed pleased with himself. He suggested I could perhaps audition for the part of the lover should his story ever be filmed. He thought that would be nifty.

Later, on the balcony with Barbara, I said: 'Patterson's quite a joker.'

She said, 'Isn't he just the greatest?'

I checked out of the hotel. The bill came to $2,653.74. I asked whether a discount couldn't be allowed. Gregory told me to forget the seventy-four cents and offered a lift. 'I'm not coming on or anything like that. I've lived with a guy called Pagan Malouf for three years now and it's seven months since we even talked about fucking,' he said, tweaking the ends of his moustache. 'We've given it up, like animal fats.'

We arrived at the apartment. I tore down the Stallone posters.

'That man has the IQ of a fence-post,' said Gregory, and when I went into the bathroom and removed the dead iguana from the toilet, holding it at arm's length, pinched between thumb and forefinger, he watched with an expression of distaste. He sighed, saying, 'I guess this could be worse. It could be in Inglewood.'

The next day I painted the living room white and pinned up a street map. I loved that map. It was coloured in soft tints of yellow, brown and orange. Santa Monica was in the West, Pasadena to the North, Pomona to the East and Anaheim to the South. The ocean was a pale blob on the left and the freeways were red ribbons like arteries. Local street names were Overland, Culver, Keystone, Coolidge, Matteson, Milton, Jefferson, Keats, Madison, Westwood, Aletta, Prospect, Empire, Fairbanks, Pickford, Garfield, Garbo, Gable, Leigh, Watseka, Tijuana, Oregon, Lasalle – Mexican names, French names, English names, historical names, names of poets and presidents and movie stars, dream names.

I wrote for bus timetables and explored the area. The MGM studios were round the corner, with buildings named after Judy Garland and David O. Selznick. There was a Ralph's supermarket and a Mexican bar called 'El As de Oros' with a huge satellite dish on the roof and a Plymouth station wagon on fire in the parking lot. It looked like a place mothers would warn their children about.

On Washington Boulevard there was a second-hand bookshop. The owner was black and middle-aged. He had a thick neck and rimless glasses. He smoked a cheroot that smelled of oranges. He told me, 'Yeah, there was this guy, some kinduvva TV evangelist up in Denver, used to come to LA once a week to record a show. One night these motherfuckers came looking for him, dressed like Klansmen but wearing real cheap robes. The guy had been saying that blacks and whites were equal in the face of God. Bad move. Real bad move. These other guys were not of that opinion. Ripped him with a machine gun, one of those soda-pop models you see in the sports classifieds, advertised by a delectable in a bikini. Zipped him in two seconds, Ba-*bing*, Ba-

bong. Whole thing went out on late night TV. Those guys come looking for me I only hope they're not wearing that cheap JC Penney shit. I want *designer* robes, man.'

'Right,' I said. It was a terrifying story. I thought it would appeal to Patterson. I imagined him blasting at me with a soda-pop machine gun, accompanied by several bikini delectables, all laughing as he sprayed bullets at my head, my chest, my penis. I imagined him smiling with mad eyes as Barbara and I hung beneath him, grasping a knife and sawing through the rope with decisive strokes, Ba-*bing*, Ba-*bong.*

'Do you have a phone?' I asked the man in the bookstore.

'Ship's Diner,' he said. 'Right across the street.'

I left, went into the restaurant, and called Barbara. She said it was difficult to talk.

'Is Patterson there?'

'I can't say anything right now.'

'Are you OK?'

'Call me in a couple of days.'

'Listen. I had this marvellous idea. Why don't we go to Mexico? Get away from it all.'

'Call me at the club.'

'Or San Francisco. I'd like to see the bridge.'

'I really can't talk right now,' she said, and hung up.

I sat in a booth and read the paper. I thought about what was happening with Barbara. Things were not working out as planned. On page thirty-six of the *LA Times* was an advertisement for Bernard Garcia, Plastic and Reconstruction Surgeon. From an office high in the eight thousands on Wilshire Mr Garcia offered Nose Improvement, Tummy Alignment, Ear Restoration, Collagen for Wrinkles, Breast Rejuvenation and Penis Harmonizing. *Perhaps it's time*, said Mr Garcia, *to make that beautiful change in your life.*

I called Takowsky. He had read my script. He said it would make a reasonable lesbian art movie. He asked if I had any other ideas.

'Some.'

'Shoot.'

'A rock star is kidnapped by terrorists, held to ransom and rescued by a teenage fan, a girl who has been taught martial arts by her mother, a widowed rape victim. She can kill with her bare hands. The fan and the star marry and go to live in Colorado.'

'Not bad.'

'A wife wants to murder her husband. But she's clever. She incriminates him for a murder. He goes to the chair, she gets the insurance.'

'How does she swing the incrimination?'

'That idea,' I said, 'is in the development stage.'

'Would the company pay out in that situation?'

'I'm not sure.'

'It sounds pretty half-baked. Nasty, and half-baked.'

'Try these. Eddie Murphy has a sex change, becomes America's first female president. Sting becomes an astronaut in a rock'n' roll version of *The Right Stuff*. Princess Diana has nightmares about Prince Charles being taken away by an evil monster and the dreams become . . . reality.'

'Keep in touch,' said Takowsky. 'These are not bad ideas, Richard. Not bad at all. But not *high concept*.'

The cook in Ship's Diner was flipping pancakes. He was lanky and his face was covered in spots. He stared as though I were soft in the head. 'Submarine movies,' he said, wiping bony, batter-covered fingers against his apron. 'You should have mentioned submarine movies. I've got this great idea for a plot about the U-boat war. You know, in the Atlantic. Convoys. Torpedoes. Red lights and machines going *ping . . . ping . . . ping*. I'll sell you the whole deal for $300. It would be perfect for Harrison Ford.'

I needed a job. 'Mechanical Man Wanted' said the sign and I went to work at the Wax Museum on Hollywood Boulevard, next to the Snow White Coffee Shop. I worked the late afternoon shift, three hours at $15 an hour. It was strange work. The first day I arrived early and met Frank. He came off at three, I went on at three-thirty. Frank was the chief mechanical man. No one cared too much about timekeeping, he said, so he took me on a tour of the museum. He laughed at the least realistic tableaux, of which there were plenty. John Wayne resembled a leering child molester. Audrey Hepburn was a wrinkled hag in a mauve dress, and in Poet's Corner Shakespeare wore a codpiece and had the awful, staring eyes of a fish left too long in the sun. Then came Bob Hope, face like an epic case of jaundice, swinging a golf club and surrounded by white-wigged footmen with candelabras and brocade coats. Frank's favourite, however, was Richard Nixon, who grinned at the centre of an assembly entitled 'The Great Presidents'. 'Just look at the guy,' Frank said, 'even in wax he's sweating like a sick whore in church.'

Frank was from Kentucky. His voice was like molasses and he called women 'poontang'. He was fifty and bald. A purple scar ran in a diagonal across the top of his head. This was the result, he said, of a golfing accident. I asked for details. He refused saying it was too painful to talk about. He was a fanatical golfer and had played all the British Open courses. As a mechanical man, he was an artist. Dressed in black tailcoat and bow tie, face gleaming with silver make-up, he could stand completely still for minutes at a stretch and an audience would gather on the black concrete pavement outside the museum, each of them convinced that Frank was a robot. That was the idea of being a mechanical man.

I wasn't very good. The first time I tried I couldn't stand still at all. My legs twitched. Frank watched from the ticket booth. He said, 'Son, don't be thinking about your body at all. Focus your eyes across the street, don't look at *them*, not even if they come right up to your face and pop chewing gum up your nose, which they probably will. Concentrate on something else. Some little piece of poontang. Or Monday night football. Or how you're gonna make a fortune. Whatever the hell you like.'

After a few days I scored my first success. I'd been a statue for about three minutes, thinking what friends in England would say if they saw me now, thinking about Barbara and what she might be doing, and then I stepped off the little wooden box on which the mechanical men stood and said, 'Good afternoon,' revealing myself human after all. Children squealed and laughed. Japanese tourists took pictures.

I'd been trying to get in touch with Barbara. When I tried the house in Hollywood Patterson answered, which meant I hung up. Each time I called the Playboy Club they said she wasn't there and they didn't know how to reach her. I left messages with Lorraine and then one morning Barbara did call, saying she and Lorraine wanted to go for a picnic in Griffith Park. I told her to pick me up at six, and they swung by in the Eldorado, Lorraine beating a jewelled hand against the bodywork, now painted day-glo pink, and saying: 'I've always wanted to have a pink Cadillac.'

'Like in the song?'

'Yeah.'

'What are you doing at the Wax Museum anyway?' said Barbara.

I said I was giving advice on English characters who might be included in the collection.

Lorraine said, 'You mean you're working as a mechanical man?'

'How did you know that?'

Barbara said, 'You saw Takowsky?'

'I wouldn't say that he's a hundred per cent sold on my ideas.'

'Takowsky, *Bow-wow-wow*sky,' she said. 'When you write a screenplay worth $575,000 he'll change his mind.' She smiled, and I wondered what made her think I could write a screenplay worth $575,000, or a screenplay worth anything at all. I caught sight of myself in the mirror, looking surprisingly eager.

'Why $575,000?' I said.

'You'd be able to buy me a new car,' mused Barbara. 'A new *pink* car. A new pink Jaguar. And a fur coat. And that cute house in Mexico.'

We stopped at a red light on Los Feliz Boulevard. Lorraine rummaged through her bag. She handed me a piece of paper, saying, 'See if this doesn't take the bleeding biscuit.'

The paper was embossed with the rabbit-head logo. It described their duties at the Playboy Club: 'When a Bunny sets napkins or drinks on the far end of a table, she does not awkwardly reach across the table – she does "The Bunny Dip". This keeps her tray away from the patrons and enables her to give graceful, stylized service. "The Bunny Dip" is performed by arching the back as much as possible then bending the knees to whatever degree is necessary. Raise the left heel as you bend the knee.' Next to the instructions was a picture of a woman in a Bunny costume, smiling and twisted into an S-shape as she performed this manoeuvre. There was more: it noted that when in view of patrons a Bunny should stand in a slightly exaggerated model's stance, with legs together, back arched, and hips tucked well under, and warned that 'The Bunny Perch' should never be executed too close to where a patron was sitting *or* on the back of his chair or sofa. It was mysterious stuff. What was 'The Bunny Perch'? *Hips tucked well under.* Well under *what*?

'Does someone really make you do this?'

'Tina gives us a test once a month,' said Barbara, and described Tina. Tina was the boss bunny. She was the one who made sure the other girls arrived on time, wore clean costumes, and didn't assault the patrons. They had to call her 'The Bunny Mother'. She sounded like a cross between Al Capone and The Chicago Bears. I imagined myself in Barbara's turquoise bunny outfit, looking for something to tuck my hips under, contorting my body in a desperate attempt to perform 'The Bunny Perch' while Bunny Mother Tina looked on, shaking her head, saying that this wouldn't do at all.

I said, 'All these rules. That's strange.'

Lorraine said, 'Yeah. But in London I worked at Burger King on the Kilburn High Road, £1.50 an hour, eight hours a day. Here I get a pink Cadillac.'

On a bridge above Vermont Avenue there were fly posters for a Tom Waits concert and two men dressed like Jake and Ellwood Blues. As we passed under the bridge the men extended their arms in a Nazi salute, shouting 'Adolf lives!'

'Oh wow,' said Barbara.

'He used to live in LA,' said Lorraine.

'Who? Adolf Hitler?'

'That geezer Tom Waits. He moved to New York when a scorpion crawled out of the shower plug and bit him on the ankle.'

'Was he hurt?'

'They rushed him to hospital.'

'It was life and death?'

'It was at the Tropicana Motel.'

The car park was filled with station wagons and Hawaiian shirts wrapped around chunky tourists. Barbara took bottles of wine from the boot and we walked towards a long, low structure in grey concrete with a blackened copper dome. This was the Griffith Observatory. Below, the city was neat squares and rectangles as far as the eye could see, with the twin towers of Century City shining in the hazy middle distance. An obelisk was carved with figures of Galileo, Kepler and Newton. Barbara smashed a wine bottle against the stone. Wine jerked from the neck and puddled on the ground.

'Forgot the corkscrew,' she said.

'Glasses?'

'Lorraine has them.'

I asked how things were going with Patterson. She said they were going fine. He'd won a bet on a college basketball game and New World looked like they were about to pick up an option on one of his screenplays. 'He's in a real great mood,' she said.

I looked through a dime telescope. I saw Barbara's house in the hills, and my own apartment. I could even pick out the rusted barbecue. 'Look at this,' I called to Barbara. She'd moved away.

We sat on a grassy bank and Lorraine poured the wine. She said, 'I got this friend and she used to be on the game. Knew this bloke and what he was into was having her stand over him with a whip and forcing him to *lick* her place clean, going round the floor and furniture with his tongue like he was a vacuum cleaner. That was what she called him. The Hoover.'

'That's sick,' said Barbara.

'It's deranged.'

'It's psycho.'

'It's . . . *the other sex.*'

'Isn't it just the truth,' said Barbara, and stared in my direction, looking me over as though I were something she'd caught and now wished to return to the water. Lorraine asked about the magazine I'd worked for in London. She'd never heard of it. I gave her the scoop. I told her about rock-star interviews, crusading news pieces, police busts, wild drug and booze orgies and mentally subnormal management who demanded cover stories featuring women in wet T-shirts.

'Of course,' I said. 'I virtually ran the place.' Lorraine looked bored.

A man threw himself on the grass. He was about fifty, with rubbery lips and a curl of black hair on his forehead. He resembled Marlon Brando playing Mark Antony in *Julius Caesar*, gone to seed. 'Do you know what happened thirty-one years ago today?' he said, gazing at Barbara. '*Do you?*'

'What's that?' I said.

He ignored me. 'Thirty-one years ago today,' he said, raping Barbara with bloodshot eyes, 'James Dean died.'

'You don't say,' she said.

'I *do* say,' he said. 'I remember like it was yesterday. I remember like it was the day Kennedy was shot. I was outside a liquor store in Neptune, New Jersey, and I heard it on the car radio. I drove across country without stopping to be here for the funeral. I've seen *Rebel Without a Cause* fifty-nine times. There is nothing about that movie which I do not love.'

'It's a pretty good movie,' said Barbara.

'It's a perfect movie.'

He told us his name was Freddy. In the 1950s he had been a teenage actor. He appeared in several movies. Then television began to destroy Hollywood and Paramount didn't pick up his option. He said, 'Jimmy and me got out of the industry about the same time. They dropped me three days after he died in the wreck.' Now he collected movie memorabilia. Occasionally there were exhibitions.

'Any money in that?' asked Barbara.

'I do OK.'

'What's the most valuable thing you've got?'

'I'd never sell any of this stuff. But the Stetson that Dean wore in *Giant*, I guess that must be worth a buttload of money, $10,000 I guess.'

Lorraine explained that she'd had a James Dean poster on her bedroom wall when she was thirteen years old. 'He was the sexiest bloke I've ever seen,' she said. Freddy smiled as though he'd discovered long-lost loved ones, and invited Lorraine and Barbara to a party where Jack Nicholson was going to be.

'Nice of you, Freddy,' I said, 'but we're all going out to dinner.'

'The party sounds neat,' said Barbara.

'The party sounds brill,' said Lorraine.

The party sounded like a nightmare.

Freddy beamed at me. 'Seems like you lost the primary,' he said. 'But I guess you can come along too.'

I went with Freddy. He drove a shit-brown Buick. Packs of Camel were strewn on the dashboard. We headed down through the park, the Eldorado following close behind.

'Crazy chicks,' he said. He bumped a cigarette from a pack and lit it. 'You friendly with the English one?'

'The other.'

'Strange, I kinda had you figured for the English chick. You being English. I sensed some kind of, some kind of real communication between you guys. On a psychic level. Know what I mean?'

I said I knew what he meant.

'And how well do you know her?'

'Which one?'

'Your one?'

'Pretty well.'

'Like *really* well?'

I said nothing, and Freddy mulled this over. He turned the Buick off Los Feliz and onto Western. 'I know that one. I mean, you never really know anyone, right? Like really *know*. What a bummer. What a total bummer.'

He held up his left hand, studied it briefly and pointed through the windscreen. 'Check those bungalows. Sometimes I get bungalonely, in the mingled human drove, and I long for bungaloafing, in some bungalotus grove.'

Freddy was way ahead of me. 'It's a poem. I've got it written on the back of my hand,' he said. 'You think I'm crazy? That's all right by me. Juju worship in Hollywood.'

Freddy swung the Buick to the left through an arch that might have been uprooted from somewhere in the Orient. We came to a stop in a courtyard. He said this was where he lived. He wanted to pick up his medication. He had a chest complaint. He was allergic to Chinese elms, he said, and he happened to live a few hundred yards away from the only known Chinese elms in the whole of Southern California. 'When the Santa Anas blow, I suffer. Guess I could live somewhere else. But I rarely venture to the west side, only to collect parts for my bicycle. Wanna come in?'

What I wanted was Freddy out of my life, but I said nothing. As I opened the car door the Eldorado pulled up behind. Lorraine and Barbara were taking turns to swig from a bottle of bourbon. Freddy said, 'Cool. Here are the chicks.'

I ran to the Eldorado. I told Barbara and Lorraine we should leave immediately. I had a bad feeling. At best Freddy was a fruitcake who wished that time had stopped in 1955. It was much more likely, I thought, that he was another character with a fondness for the long, sharp hunting knife. 'Oh, Richard,' said Barbara, 'don't be so uptight,' and strode down a path towards Freddy. He opened the door of a bungalow and beckoned her inside. I followed.

The room was painted blood-red. Furniture and carpet were the same colour and red blinds eliminated daylight. It was like walking into someone else's body. 'Just think of him,' said Freddy in a quiet voice. 'Thirty-one years ago today.'

An entire wall was covered by a blown-up photo of the twisted wrecked Porsche in which Dean died. Another was illuminated by a red neon sign flashing, *Jet . . . Rink, Jet . . . Rink, Jet . . . Rink.* On a table was a three-foot-high James Dean doll, cigarette dangling from the lips, which Freddy said was 'very rare, very valuable', perhaps even more valuable than the Stetson from *Giant* which, I saw, was in a corner on an altar table next to a framed icon of the star, inscribed with the words 'James Dean, born Fairmount, Indiana, 1931 – His Flesh Will Never Die'. Electric candles surrounded the altar table, flickering red light.

Freddy moved to and fro, gesturing towards items in his collection. Here was Sal Mineo's knife from *Rebel*, here was a lettuce box from *East of Eden*, here was a handkerchief which Elizabeth Taylor had used in *Giant*. He handed me a book.

He said, 'Unique edition of the screenplay for *Rebel Without a Cause*.'

'The covers feel strange,' I said, and they did, warm and silky.

Freddy grinned: 'Bound in human skin.'

We were in a polished steel railway car converted to a bar on Santa Monica Boulevard. I asked Barbara how dangerous she thought Freddy had been really. She said nothing. Lorraine laughed so hard she choked on her Bloody Mary. 'You should have seen Richard when he came out of that place,' she said. 'His jacket was flapping up by his ears. His eyes were popping out of his head. He looked like a terrified bat.'

'I wasn't staying,' I said. 'That bloke Freddy had both paddles out of the water. Big league madness.'

'Shame about that party, though. Now I can only say, "I met Jack Nicholson, *nearly*".'

Barbara said, 'Sometimes I think LA is just a nightclub. It's four in the morning and nobody wants to go home.' She took a plate. She sent it skimming like a frisbee with a smooth action of the wrist. The plate curved past three or four people's heads, hovered and smashed against the bar. She picked up another plate. This one struck the chest of a man who had just come through the door. Barbara said, 'Let's party.'

Heads turned. The barman reached for a phone.

'Jesus. What did you do that for?'

'I hate this town.'

'You're always telling me how much you love LA.'

Barbara turned sideways in the booth and faced the wall. She began to cry. I asked what was the matter and she said nothing. I thought: what next? Perhaps Barbara would announce she was Cleopatra reincarnated and had to catch the midnight flight to Cairo. It had been a confusing night.

A man loomed over me, pungent with the smell of sweat. He was nearly seven feet tall and his wobbling belly was restrained by a Bon Jovi T-shirt. His ham-like fist descended on my shoulder. 'You throw that plate, pal?' he said. His voice made it clear this was a statement rather than a question. He advised us to leave.

Lorraine rang the next day. I was at the Wax Museum. Barbara had flown to Maui for two weeks. She had asked Lorraine to give me the message.

'*Maui?*'

'It's in Hawaii.'

'I know where it is.'

'She's sorry she couldn't get in touch with you. It's an assignment, came up at the last minute. One of the other girls dropped out. Barbara said you'd know the photographer.'

'Michael?'

'That's the geezer.'

'Is this for real?'

Lorraine said it was for real, and asked if I wanted to see Ry Cooder at the Palace later in the week. Chuck had free tickets.

'Barbara's crazy about you,' she said. I asked what evidence she had to support this assertion.

I got to know Los Angeles. I got to know one of my neighbours. He had a wispy goatee beard and hair which stood up vertically. There were bags beneath his eyes the size of snooker-table pockets, and he wore very pointed shoes made from alligator skin. He looked like he had walked off the set of a beatnik movie. He introduced himself one night, asking if I had any rat poison.

'I have these rats in my apartment,' he said. He had a deep, rasping voice. 'Lemme tell you about these rats. They're huge and dark, they're massive and subtle. I've beaten them over the head, I've put broken bottles in their holes and I've fed them with the poison I got until they're fat like Elizabeth Taylor. Maybe there's something wrong with the poison. They just come back for more. Maybe these are special animals. A new breed of super rat. You got any rats?'

'No,' I said, 'iguana.'

'*Iguana*,' he said, examining a scuff on the point of one of his shoes. 'That's an angle.'

My neighbour was called Wallace Moss. He was a musician, trying to get a record contract. I went with him to buy some beer from the Davy Jones Liquor Locker on Sepulveda. It was nine at night and a cool breeze came off the ocean. He said, 'I was down on the beach a coupla days back, in Venice, and I saw this woman, this totally *bald* woman and I'm telling you she'd lost it. She had pages of the *Examiner* wrapped round her legs and there was a bottle of sour mash in her hands. She was singing, "Raindrops . . . ya fuckin mother . . . keep fallin on my head . . . ya pig, ya fuckin cunt . . . but that doesn't mean . . . ya fuck . . . my eyes will soon be turnin *red* ya fuckin fuck . . . *red* . . . nothin seems to fit . . . fucker." And then she just went out. Keeled over right in the street. Bang. I've never heard anyone treat a Burt Bacharach song in quite that way before. It made it real for me, you know. That's what I want to do, end up as a part of the fabric, write a song that becomes part of the life that goes on around me. Then I'll die happy.'

The Davy Jones Liquor Locker was like a fortress, with a massive steel door, bars on the windows, and a security guard with a revolver and nightstick at the hip. Moss asked why I was in Los Angeles. I told him I'd met a girl. I showed him a picture which Barbara and I had posed for in a booth on the pier at Santa Monica.

I said, 'She's engaged. Sort of.'

'To you?'

'No.'

'No?'

'No.'

'I see,' he said. 'How's it going?'

'She's in Hawaii.'

Moss rolled his eyes. He said he thought I needed to get this straightened out. He had a theory about passion. 'It's a disease which affects two people. Sooner or later one of them turns into a monster.' The security guard said he also had a theory about passion. We didn't stay to listen to it. We bought two six-packs of Rolling Rock and went back to my apartment.

Moss sprawled on the floor, breathing loudly, bottled poised on his chest. He asked what was the first movie I ever saw. I thought for a few seconds.

'*The Dam Busters*. British war movie. We bomb the Krauts.'

'First record you ever owned?'

'*Come On*. A present from my brother.'

'Stones or Chuck Berry?'

'Stones. And you?'

Moss had liked Johnny Mercer, Jerome Kern, Duke Ellington, T. Rex – the usual crowd. He grew up in Los Angeles, El Paso, Denver, Phoenix and Michigan. His family, like my own, moved around. He remembered lullabies, and his father singing 'Molly Malone', and hearing Mexican dance songs on the radio in the pick-up they had. He always wanted to be a musician. At school he played a bugle given to him by his father, a Cleveland Greyhound. He played when the flag was raised in the morning and when it was lowered in the afternoon. He could still remember the smell of the bugle case: bad eggs and a stale T-shirt.

I thought about my own father. I remembered when he owned the second of his garage businesses and drove me to school in a different car each day. One day it would be a Sunbeam Alpine, the next an Aston Martin, the day after that a clapped-out Morris Oxford. Once we rolled up in a Daimler hearse. He always said only three things mattered in life: sex, Frank Sinatra and cricket, not just any cricket, but *Yorkshire* cricket. He was a fanatic. He thought Freddie Trueman was God on earth. I was at college when my father was discovered in a fraud. It was a lot of money,

I'm not sure exactly how much, but a lot, and he went to jail, an open prison near Preston. I saw him there. He'd lost a lot of weight and was unrepentant. He was making another fortune in prison because he didn't smoke and could trade his tobacco ration for all sorts of other stuff. He told me he'd become a sort of prison baron. He also told me how he'd once stolen Patrick MacGoohan's girlfriend. That was in the 1960s, after my mother had divorced him, when MacGoohan was a famous actor, star of a secret-agent TV series called *Danger Man*. My father was in a pub in London and MacGoohan came in with a tall and attractive woman, a blonde. MacGoohan went to the bar for drinks and my father made his move. He said to the woman: 'You don't want to stay with him do you?' MacGoohan came back and was very angry. He wanted a fight. My father said, 'Fuck off, Danger Man,' and to his surprise Danger Man did precisely that. He then took the woman to a hotel, some place near Regent's Park. They stayed in bed for two days. Sex, for my father, was a matter of fierce, if sometimes temporary, attachments.

'You got work?' said Moss. He rolled an empty beer bottle across the floor.

'Of sorts. The Hollywood Wax Museum.'

'As a mechanical man?'

'Why does everybody know that?'

'A buddy of mine tried it. He lasted nine days. You had a job at home?'

'I was a journalist.'

'They fired you?'

'I didn't tell them when I came here.'

'You just walked out?'

I nodded.

'Oh, man,' said Moss. 'Have penis, will travel.'

I had time on my hands. I went with Moss to Nadine's Music Store in Hollywood. He sat on a piano stool and fingered a 1959 Fender Stratocaster, coal-fire red and inlaid with mother of pearl. He said he had dreamed of owning a guitar like this since he was a child and saw a film of Buddy Holly. He took a plectrum and picked out the chords to 'True Love Ways'. His style was flamboyant rather than accurate. Moss asked when Barbara was coming back from Hawaii. I said I wasn't sure. I was trying not to think about it. With Barbara gone, I was not sure what I was doing in Los Angeles. With Barbara gone, I worried about money. The news wasn't good.

The last time I'd tried my Mastercard it had been confiscated by a cashier in Lucky's who looked at me like I was a sex offender and treated me to several minutes' abuse for trying to use the card while in such massive excess of my credit limit. I was scared to use my American Express because I hadn't paid a bill in two months. Being a mechanical man barely covered living expenses. I had to find something for the mornings or evenings, something which paid much better. While we'd been at the château Barbara had told me how she once earned $100 a night waiting table at the Hamburger Hamlet on San Vicente. I went there on the RTD bus to see the manager. He was friendly, and showed me his waiting list. It was almost as long as the one for people who wanted to be extras in the new Spielberg movie. I knew about that because I'd been to a casting call at a hotel on Melrose. A skinny man with a nose like a crushed strawberry had told me I was the wrong physical type. When I'd asked him to elaborate he'd informed me that if I didn't leave *right now* he would send for security. It was a problem.

Moss returned the guitar to a stand. We walked out of the store and up Vine St towards Sunset. There was a white concrete building like something ripped from a radio: Capitol Records, said Moss, they still had one of his demo tapes. 'Only way to get them to listen is to go in and press a gun to some executive's head. That's the way Little Anthony and the Imperials did it.'

A black Porsche roadster slid by, engine rumbling, with the registration plate 'ALL NOW' and a girl at the wheel who looked sixteen years old. She waved, and Moss groaned, kicking an alligator shoe against an empty Coke can on the pavement. 'This is no town to be poor. Every minute someone goes by in their dream car, with their dream life, rubbing your face in it, every minute of every day,' he said.

I was getting the hang of being a mechanical man. There were no more derisive stares. My calves were used to the strain of standing on the box. Frank said that pretty soon I'd be as good as him. Frank was a fan of the *Hollywood Press*, a seventy-five-cent tabloid which carried outlandish, scary lonely-hearts messages, pornographic photos so smudgy and indistinct they might have been beamed from Mars, and sleazy tales of medicine and murder. There was a staff room at the Wax Museum. It lay behind a door marked 'Danger – High Explosive', next to the Chamber of Horrors. Frank was there each afternoon after his shift, chuckling over this paper. One day he showed me a story:

SURGEON APPALLED BY DRACULA CLAIM

An elderly man who believed he had been bitten in the neck by the vampire Dracula while walking his dog in Buena Vista Park asked a surgeon to drive a stake through his heart when he died, the American Medical Defence Union revealed yesterday. John Gordon, an English ex-actor and stunt man, died two months ago aged 63, warning that he too would become a vampire and rise from the dead if his instructions were not carried out. The surgeon in the case, Dr Miller Fong, consulted AMDU lawyers who informed him he was under no obligation to conform with the macabre request. The family of John Gordon is now claiming $5m damages. The dead man's daughter, Mary Beth Gordon, said: 'This was my Dad's final request. It was their duty to comply with it. He knew that evil lived in this world. Now he too walks at night, seeking peace for his soul. Dr Fong behaved disgracefully. He lied to my father. He sent my father to Hell.'

I said, 'That's a great story.'
Frank said, 'I love that kind of stuff.' He revealed that he himself had once been the subject of a *Hollywood Press* exposé.

He looked at me like he wanted me to tell him I didn't believe him. I told him I didn't believe him. 'It's the plain truth,' he said. He explained. Back in Kentucky he had specialized in armed robbery. He had been good at it, made a lot of money. He went wrong when he started working with the brother of his ex-wife. The family came from Yugoslavia, or one of those Communist countries, Frank said. 'Not that I know much about Communism, but the first couple of jobs, they went fine. Then one day we're taking down this fancy restaurant in Louisville, right around the time of Derby Day, everything's going as slick as you like, and suddenly the kid, my partner, he's screaming at everybody, telling them to take off their clothes. I'm looking at the kid, asking him "What the hell's going on here?" and he's holding his automatic to some poontang's head telling her to *remove* her dress. The kid is definitely having some kind of major mental bugaboo, like he's *flipped*, and I'm beginning to realize the only way I'm ever gonna get him out of there is if I shoot him and I can't do that 'cos he's family and so I go over, tag him on the shoulder and try to be reasonable. And what does he do? He kicks me in the nuts. So I've got my ass on the floor and my balls in my hand and the kid's down there as well, trying to get himself some spare with this poontang, and the law arrives. Officer said it was the strangest arrest he ever made.'

Frank said he was in all the papers, including the *Hollywood Press*. Then he was in the state penitentiary, for five years. He had the cuttings at home. He would bring them in to show me, if I wanted. 'Sometimes I even think about going back into the business,' he said, 'if I could find myself the right partner.' He gave me a sly look. Did he mean what I thought he meant? Was he serious? In his mind was I already transformed into Rayner the reliable, Rayner the one with no mental bugaboos, Rayner, Hold-Up Man? It was a scary thought.

'I could never do it,' I said. 'The accent. Dead give-away.'

'Son,' said Frank. 'Think about it. In this world there are more horses' asses than horses. Which do *you* want to be?'

I went for a job cleaning swimming pools.

The first thing the man did was to give me a uniform: white pumps and socks, white Bermuda shorts, white vest and a white nylon zipper jacket with 'Clean Blue Yonder' stitched on the back in thread coloured azure, like an Italian football shirt. The man was called McCrea. He was big, about 6′ 4″, with bushy eyebrows and a jutting chin. His chest might have been cut to fit Arnold Schwarzenegger, and he had the habit of stretching his neck forward, as if he were about to start clucking, like a chicken. Clean Blue Yonder was his creation. 'You see, Richard,' he said, 'we don't have inclement weather here in Los Angeles. God understands that we don't want to handle it emotionally. So He has given us the sun, and He has given us the swimming pools.' He gripped my shoulder with sausage-like fingers and leaned his vast head close to mine. 'God also understands that people don't want dirt in their swimming pools. That's why he told me to start Clean Blue Yonder. It's my mission.'

Clean Blue Yonder was on Sepulveda Boulevard. Opposite was a monstrous red-brick construct which housed the world's biggest health club, with uniformed doormen, and valet parking. McCrea's centre of operations was more modest. The building was squat, the interior cramped. There was a tiny cubicle at the back. McCrea stood outside while I changed.

He said, 'I do a lot of swimming and when I see a dirty pool, or one with too much chlorine, or one where the sweep isn't working properly, I get so mad I want to take the owner and just stare his ass down. Sometimes I get so mad I want to hit people. I have to ask Him for patience.'

The cubicle had a mirror. A poster on the wall said: 'Bayside prophecy – Jesus and Mary speak to the world through Marlene McCrea'. The poster noted: '*All who condone homosexuality, abortion, shall be destroyed*. As Jesus said on June 2, 1979, "And I repeat again: all who become part of or condone homosexuality shall be destroyed! All who become part of or condone abortion, the murder of the young, *shall be destroyed*! All who seek to cast out the discipline given by the Eternal Father in the Commandments, The Ten Commandments from your God – they too shall be destroyed! All women who disport their bodies in nakedness, *the flesh shall burn*." '

As Jesus said . . . on *June 2, 1979?* It seemed that the Son of Galilee had become a vengeful character. The poster warned that devastating earthquakes would soon strike California. I pulled on white shorts and imagined the catastrophe: people drowned, bodies crushed, and Los Angeles flattened, a heap of collapsed brick and glass with fires burning in the debris. I wondered if the swimming pools would be spared. Perhaps these days Jesus swam in the water, rather than walking upon it.

I saw myself in the mirror. My legs were weak and spindly, my flesh almost as white as the uniform. I resembled the Mr Softee Man. I stepped out and McCrea grinned, showing huge teeth. 'Looking good, looking sharp,' he said. He said that for the first few days I'd be going out with Norris. 'I wish I could take you out myself,' he said, stretching his jaw forward, 'but Norris is a good kid, a capable kid, he'll show you the ropes. His attitude towards swimming pools is wholesome. He respects swimming pools.'

The man who respected swimming pools was small and muscular, with black, wiry hair. 'Norris, I want you to meet Richard. He's the latest of our angels,' said McCrea. 'I want you to take him out with you. Who's on the list today?'

'Silas, Wechsler and Murchison.'

'Anything difficult?'

'Wechsler sounds like a bummer.'

'Gee, that woman can be a trial. But we've got to learn to handle situations like that. We must have patience.'

'What can I tell ya, dude? You're right.'

I wondered whether to tell McCrea something. The ad in the *LA Weekly* – 'Wanted, Angels of the Poolside, hours flexible' – had required the possession of a valid California driver's licence. I hadn't mentioned that I didn't drive, and McCrea hadn't asked. I decided to skip it.

McCrea stretched forward his jaw again. 'I'll leave you boys to it. Richard,' he said, 'the Lord be with you.'

Norris took me outside. 'McCrea tell you about his mission from God?' he said.

'He did mention it once or twice.'

'Is that one wild and crazy dude, or what?'

'Who's Marlene?'

'His wife. Just wait till you meet her, dude. Look into both their eyes, it's like empty, no one at home. He's just crazy. She should have her own TV show. That lady can *talk*.'

We loaded equipment into a white Honda van. 'Clean Blue Yonder' was painted on the side. Norris inspected my legs with an expression of disbelief. He said, 'You the athletic type?'

We drove up Sepulveda, headed east on Olympic. Norris told me he was from Pasadena and had dropped out of UCLA. His ambition was to move south to Orange County and work in the Hobie Surf Shop at Dana Point. He said 'dude', pronounced *dood*, a lot and reckoned he might even take a shot at professional surfing. His idol was Tommy Carroll. He said, 'Dudes like that, they're totally dialled in. They can earn a quarter of a million a year, serious coin. But it's not the money. You're out on your board at Huntington, there's a light wind coming off the point and the waves are glassy, corduroy as far as you can see. You hear the water splash against the board and then you're up, blowing some other guy off the wave, diving down, cutting a turn, stepping to the end of a board, noseriding. It's perfect, dude, that's life.' He asked me about London. He wanted to visit. He'd heard it was a totally happening place, except for the surfing.

We were in Beverly Hills. The streets were deserted. Norris steered the van through a gate and we went down a crescent-shaped gravel drive and pulled up in front of a large house. The house was imitation Tudor, black and white, with tall gables. The pool was round the back. Norris fixed a loose filter on the hot tub, while I trawled the pool with a device which resembled a butterfly net. I caught leaves, the lower half of a bikini, and several empty bottles of San Pellegrino. I told Norris about Barbara.

'Surfer chick?'

'Not as far as I know.'

This puzzled him. 'Why else would anyone go to Hawaii?' he said.

The next job was up in Bel Air, on Bellagio Road, at a white house on the side of a hill. The house was built on stilts, and built upside down. We went in through the kitchen, down a flight of stairs with hunting prints on the walls, past the bedroom, down another flight into the living area which was decorated in dark wood like a ship's cabin with compasses and charts, and out into a big garden. Everything in the garden was laid out with care. There were flower beds, palm trees with trimmed branches, and lots of statues of Napoleon. These came in various shapes and sizes and I counted twenty-three, not including the one on the red-tiled bottom of the swimming pool. This one was very large and broken into eight pieces, each piece magnified and distorted by the water.

An old woman stood at the pool's edge. She was red-faced and tall. She wore a battered straw hat. She hadn't seemed to acknowledge our arrival but she began to speak, in a German accent, saying: 'You are late. You will remove him now. Lynch will attend to the repairs, later.'

Norris stared down.

'What happened here, Mrs Wechsler? I thought you guys liked Napoleon? You go crazy, stage a revolution?'

'Just do the work, if you please. And try not to damage the statue.'

'That's gonna be tough, Mrs Wechsler. We'll do our best.'

'Make sure you do.'

We went to the van for tools and equipment. Norris said, 'Shit, that woman's such a tight-ass.' He said he had been to this house several times before. Once Mrs Wechsler had told him she worked as a secretary in the administration block of a concentration camp. 'You know, those dudes in Nazi Germany,' said Norris. He had asked her what it was like. She had said the hours were long.

'Is that true?'

'This is Beverly Hills, dude. I'll believe anything.'

We were back in the garden. I watched Mrs Wechsler as she attacked a bush with shears. I tried to imagine her typing papers and filing forms in some grey room in Dachau or Auschwitz.

'One of us is going to get soaked,' said Norris. 'And it's not going to be me. I only go into water with a wet suit.' He clamped a pulley to the edge of the pool. I dived and fixed nets to each piece of the broken statue. I fixed ropes to the nets. I got out of the pool and we hauled up the pieces one by one.

'They're not really going to be able to fix this, are they?' I said as we heaved out another large, and particularly heavy, chunk.

'Beats me, too,' he said.

It was dark when we finished. A strong wind goose-bumped my flesh, and Norris said: 'I've seen some weird shit doing this job. Went to this house up on Mulholland one time, guy had a red Freightliner truck in his pool. Never found out how the thing got there. Another time, in the Palisades, there was this woman, her husband was in the military, she kept a dolphin in her pool, said it had been trained to kill by the CIA. Like I said, crazy people.'

Moss and I went to the Ry Cooder show with Lorraine and her boyfriend Chuck, the A&R man at Warner Bros. Chuck wore a red leather jacket and the same white silk trousers he had on when I first met him. He also wore a hat like a matador's, which came halfway down his forehead. We were in the Palace Theatre, at Hollywood and Vine, and Chuck didn't look out of place. The bar was a fashion show: men with Robert de Niro stubble, women with short, backless dresses in gold and silver, women with teased Christie Brinkley hairstyles, and teenage girls who said they were from the Valley and came in the boyfriend's BMW, and must have changed in a garage restroom somewhere, since their parents surely wouldn't let them come out looking like *that*. Faces turned to check new arrivals as they came down the stairs, in case they were famous.

'He's so great. His work changed my life. He's the kind of writer I'd give my life to be,' a man near the bar told his friends.

'I hear he's at Grey now, Caesar's Palace account,' someone else said.

'Isn't that the same guy who wrote the Alaska Airline commercial?' said a third.

'That's the guy . . .'

'He's some kinduvva genius.'

'*Caesar's*. Wow, what an opportunity . . .'

'Yeah. One day you're just a guy, the next day the sun rises and falls . . .'

Chuck returned from the bar, carrying a tray loaded with bottles of Heineken. 'Eh, *voila* . . .,' he said. Moss interrogated him about what he had to do to land a recording contract. Chuck said, 'Tough one, Wallace, tough one. We did just sign "Duane's Addiction". Killer band. Sorta glam-rock, sorta heavy-metal, sorta post-punk. Real original. Right, baby?'

'Right, Chuck,' said Lorraine.

A vein swelled on Moss's forehead.

I said to Lorraine, 'So Barbara's crazy about me?'

'That's what I said.'

'And that's why she went to Hawaii?'

She suggested I put myself in Barbara's place. On the one hand there was Patterson, who was a little bit odd, a little bit *strange*, and on the other there was this Englishman who she'd only met for about five minutes on a Greek island and had suddenly arrived on the doorstep and wouldn't leave her alone and was working as a *mechanical man*.

I said I also cleaned swimming pools.

'Give her a break,' said Lorraine. I stared at her. The exaggerated Cockney accent had disappeared. She looked defiant. 'Yeah, I puts that on for the punters, don't I?'

I gulped down several Heinekens. I felt drunk. Bryan Ferry of Roxy Music stood at the back, watching the show. I went and introduced myself. He was puzzled, and polite. He said he was in Los Angeles to make a record. He was living in the Malibu colony house which had once belonged to Fritz Lang. I told him a story about a friend of mine, a film-maker who loved Lang's work and came to Los Angeles to interview him. This was in the 1970s, not long before Lang died. Somehow my friend never got round to the interview. He felt the city had robbed him of his will.

Ferry smiled. I told him I thought 'Can't Let Go', a song he'd recorded when Jerry Hall was dumping him for Mick Jagger, was one of the best things written about LA: *'They said go west young man that's best, it's there you'll feel no pain, Bel-Air's okay if you dig the grave, but I want to live again.'* I told him I thought the song was very good on the experience of feeling rootless in a foreign place. He looked embarrassed. I told him I was an Englishman, having a bit of woman trouble myself.

He smiled again. He obviously thought I was wrong in the head. But the judgement of a man who had once appeared in public wearing toreador pants was not to be trusted.

Norris told me he had just turned twenty-seven.

'I thought you were younger.'

He said, 'Life's passing me by, dude, and that's fine by me.' Norris had been a baseball star at UCLA, an outstanding hitter and a good outfielder, due for a try-out with the California Angels when his car ran off the Pasadena Freeway in the wet and he hurt his wrist. He hadn't played baseball since. 'Happened on the worst stretch of freeway in the city. They built it way back in the 1920s and they thought they'd better put in all these totally steep curves. In case people got bored. Can you believe it? To cause chaos, all you need is a coupla buckets of water.' He said he didn't mind not being able to play baseball. He hated the idea of becoming someone whose life was shattered because something went wrong when he was twenty-one. He said, 'This dude I know, I call him The Hoop Casualty. It's like he's still in shock, trying to get over the fact that he didn't quite make it to the NCAA finals. Dude, I tell ya, soon as I get things together I'm gone from this LA shit. I'm heading down to Dana. The beach. Never go east of Coast Highway if I can possibly help it.'

We were on Mapleton Drive. Norris turned the van through

gates flanked by thick hedges with purple leaves. The house was long and low, and white. It had a red-tile roof, and a pair of Chinese dragons at the door. We went round the side. A man wearing a pith helmet was crouched on the path, adjusting sprinklers. Water hissed, and spread in fan-shaped patterns across the lawn.

'Who owns this place?' I asked.

'Some guy in the movies,' said Norris. 'Who cares?'

The pool was shaped like a kidney and tiled in squares of blue and gold. There was a diving board, and a red rubber ring bobbed on the water. While we tested for acidity Norris tried to explain some inscrutable aspect of surfing, something about the difference between inside and outside waves. *An inside wave.* I didn't understand at all. We cleaned the filters and Norris said, 'You're not getting this, are you?'

'No,' I said.

'An outside wave . . .' he began. But before he could say any more the pool-sweep began to behave strangely. Two of the hoses which creep along the bottom, sucking up debris, suddenly came out of the pool and shot water in the air. Within moments we were drenched.

'Great,' said Norris. 'That's great.'

We got the sweep out of the pool. We tried to turn it off. This was not easy. I recalled a film in which John Wayne wore a diving helmet and wrestled an octopus. Our task was similar. Each time we thought we'd cracked it, another length of hose would break loose and give us a soaking. Norris was like a dog being given a wash. 'No wet suit,' he moaned. At last he found the switch, and, with a final twitch, the pool sweep died.

A man came across the lawn. The gardener touched his pith helmet as he passed. The man ignored him. He was small and fat and wore garish yellow beach shorts. His nose was swollen, as if he'd been stung by a bee. 'Say, you guys are soaked,' he said, chuckling. 'You gonna be able to fix this thing?'

'We'll have to take it away,' said Norris.

'Won't hear me complaining. Thing drives me nuts. Don't see the point of it.'

I saw a woman standing on the patio outside the house. She was tall and wore a black swimsuit. She was looking up at the roof, perhaps she'd seen something. I stared at her: long legs, long fair hair, tanned back. It was Barbara.

'Hey,' I shouted. 'Barbara. Isn't this a surprise.' It struck me how I hated coincidence in fiction: chance meetings like this, or those scenes where a man finds a letter written by his wife, a letter to her lover which just happens to fall from her pocket. 'How was Hawaii?'

The woman faced me. She was incredibly beautiful, and she was not Barbara.

'My name's not . . .'

'Excuse me,' I said. 'My mistake.'

She shrugged. 'That's OK.'

'Terrible eyesight.'

'No problem.'

The man in the yellow shorts was baffled. He scrutinized me, he scrutinized the woman. 'Lemme get this right. You know the poolman?'

'No, I don't.'

'She doesn't.'

'I'm all turned around here.'

'I thought she was someone else. It was a silly mistake.'

It was no use. The man in the yellow beach shorts was off and running. He had formed his paranoid theory. 'You actually know . . . *the poolman*. You actually come on to the poolman while I'm here. After what happened last week. You disgust me.'

The woman said she wasn't going to listen to this. She went back into the house. The man in the yellow beach shorts ran after her, still shouting, 'Bitch! You disgust me.'

When we had packed away our equipment, Norris said: 'Dudely chick, man.'

I tried calling Barbara. Patterson answered. 'I know who this is,' he said, 'so please don't hang up.'

I said nothing.

'So. How's it going?'

'I'm OK.'

'When did you last see Barbara?'

I told him this was none of his business.

'I want you to keep away from her. Don't see her. Don't talk to her. Don't even think about it.'

'Don't be ridiculous.'

'*Stay away!*' he shouted. '*Just stay the fuck away from her.*'

I went round to Moss's apartment. He laughed when I told him about the phone call. 'You talk about your life like it was a movie,' he said. He showed me a cupboard. Inside was a mountainous heap of alligator shoes. There were alligator shoes of all descriptions: alligator boots, with and without zips; alligator shoes with laces, and ones which slipped on; and alligator shoes with all varieties of heel (cuban, platform, stacked, flat).

'How many pairs do you have?'

'Not,' said Moss, 'as many as I'd like.'

The RTD bus was the usual collection: an oldster wobbling from the step-well on bent legs, a Mexican leafing desperately through immigration forms, a cripple on sticks held together with Band-Aid, a driver who sniffed and scowled in response to any enquiry, and the bad boys at the back, laughing and smoking dope, singing along to Prince on the ghetto blaster, outdoing each other with stories of how long it took them to travel to work each day: two hours, three hours, three hours-forty. One said, 'I wanna sleep for ever. Why get up?'

'You'll get up, sucker,' said one of the others. 'Otherwise your boss'll stick his dick up your ass.'

On Wilshire a red Golf convertible went by, a bronze hulk at the wheel, one arm thrown carelessly round the shoulder of a blonde in the passenger seat. He whispered in her ear and she laughed. Stickers on the bumper said 'Wine Me, Dine Me, 69 Me' and 'GO GO GO USC.'

'Oh, man,' said one of the bad boys, groaning. 'Check that chick.'

'There's a USC in *sucks*,' said another.

'Fucking USC. The University of *Spoiled Children*, man.'

The bus smashed down an incline, thumping and rattling. At the end of Wilshire the Pacific rose up like a blue wall. I opened a window. Air smelling of ocean and used tyres poured in.

'You went to college?' said Barbara.

I nodded.

'Where?'

'Cambridge.'

'What was it like?'

'USC, but English.'

'What was your major?'

'Philosophy.'

'We read some of that stuff in the twelfth grade,' she said. She guessed it hadn't changed much.

I felt pole-axed. Barbara had come to the apartment. She hadn't brought the car, she said, because she was afraid Patterson would try to follow her. She had told him she was stepping out for a jog. She was wearing tracksuit bottoms and white T-shirt. Her hair was taken up behind her head in a bun. She had said she hadn't been in Hawaii. She was sorry for the lie, but she had needed time to think. She had smiled, and suggested we go to the beach.

The bus thumped down another slope. It stopped.

'Maybe I should have gone to college,' said Barbara.

'What stopped you?'

'I was with this guy. That was in Buffalo when Patterson and I split for a while. He was older than me. He was about forty, I guess. Really brilliant guy. He could have taught stuff. He knew about everything. Not just history and books. On a train he'd stare at people's feet and tell me exactly what they were like just from looking at their shoes. We travelled. Went to Japan and Egypt and Morocco. It was a crazy year. He started to drink. Turned out he had another girlfriend, in New York. He went back to her. We met at the funeral. His drinking had gotten worse and worse. He tried to get her to sleep with his friends. She wouldn't. He walked out of a twenty-sixth storey window. Killed himself. He did it while she was still in the room.'

The bus started up. A man came down the aisle. He had dark glasses and a wrinkled neck like a turkey. 'Excuse *me*,' he said. His breath was the smell of garlic and he started to talk as though he'd just walked onto a stage. 'I wouldn't want you to get the wrong idea,' he said. 'I never approach men for any reason whatsoever. My aim is to find girls, beautiful girls who are alone and preferably over-sexed.' I wondered how he decided about the over-sexed bit. 'I go to singles bars, try to pick up girls. You'd be surprised how often I go to singles bars. Lately I've been unlucky.' He examined Barbara and, literally, licked his lips. 'But maybe my luck's about to change.'

'What's your problem, buddy?' she said.

'Problem? Lady, I've got more than my share in that department. Three years ago I got hit by a car in Reno, lost my mobility.' He smiled, as though this were a splendid joke: what a wheeze – *get crippled*. 'Lost lots of other things to tell the truth but my mobility was the most important. Now I've gotta get back east. That's my priority. The singles bars back east.'

The bus came to a halt. 'We passed 19th St yet?' he asked. 'I got an appointment with this video dating agency. You go in and they shoot you on video. Women pick you out. I'm meeting one today. Shit, this *is* 19th St.' He pushed his way to the exit.

'Go home and die, creepo,' shouted Barbara.

We got off the bus at Santa Monica. The bad boys at the back whistled and jeered. It was sunny and warm. Lollipop palm trees swayed in the wind. Sailboats bobbed on the ocean and to the north waves beat against Santa Monica Point, jutting into the bay like the snout of a dinosaur. A man was in front of us, pushing a supermarket trolley loaded with rags and empty bottles. He stumbled in high-heeled cowboy boots. The sole of the left boot slapped against the concrete. He wiped a greasy hand through his beard, muttering, 'I can do it, I can do it, I can do it, *really* I can do it.' There were lots of bums here. As Hooter (or was it Jack?) had said, this was where America stopped. A graffito on the Will

Rogers esplanade said: 'Welcome to the end of civilization'. People arrived, and many didn't move on. There they were, lying beneath the palm trees, wrapped in newspapers and old sweaters and sleeping bags, contemplating the Pacific like characters from a Jack Kerouac story.

I asked Barbara why she had come to Los Angeles. She said she came with Patterson when he graduated from Columbia and tried for a job at Spielberg's Amblin' Films. He nearly got the job, but didn't, and enrolled on a screenwriting course. There hadn't seemed much point in her going back to Buffalo, so she started waiting tables. They had lived in an apartment on Kiowa Avenue, then she saw an ad in *Variety* for the house on Venus Drive in the hills. They had moved there about a year ago. 'I met Lorraine and went to work at the club. Then Kimberley ran away to Europe and Mom sent me to bring her back. I met you. And that's the whole story,' said Barbara.

We walked over a footbridge to the pier. There was a carousel, painted in red and brilliant yellow. Riderless horses swung round and round, jerking to accompaniment from a Wurlitzer. I knew they'd filmed part of *The Sting* here, the scene at the beginning before Paul Newman has met Robert Redford.

'What's going to happen with us?'

'I don't know, Richard.'

'Leave Patterson.'

The ticket collector leaned against a booth. He was thin and looked angry. 'I'll tell you something for nothing,' he said. 'Paul Newman's a faggot.' He grinned, displaying horrid, pointy teeth.

'I didn't know that.'

'Do now.'

'I thought he'd been happily married for years.'

'You thought wrong. What I hear, he don't even swing both ways.' He leaned forward, wanting to confide something. He said, 'Hershey bars. And Robert Redford's a fucking Republican.'

I took Barbara outside. On the pier a short Mexican in a leather cowboy hat argued with the woman who ran the leaping frogs game. She spoke in a loud voice and looked like something from an opera by Wagner. The Mexican had a grievance. He gestured angrily towards the game, the idea of which was to place a frog in a device resembling a miniature siege catapult, then whack the other end of the device with a steel hammer, thus launching the frog towards a pond. There were lilies in the pond and if the frog landed on one, the prize was a cuddly toy. The Mexican felt he'd been deprived of his prize. Unless he got a cuddly toy, he said, there would be trouble, revenge, bloodshed.

I asked Barbara when she thought she might make up her mind about leaving Patterson.

She said, 'Are those frogs *alive?*'

We went down steps to the shore. Barbara watched kids racing across the beach. She said that in her teens she had been New York State champion in the 800 metres. She nearly made the national team. 'I miss the training,' she said. 'I miss the routine. I used to work at it real hard. Training every day, races once a week. I had a focus.'

We took off our shoes and lay on the sand. The sunset was spectacular, changing colour every minute: red, pink, orange, lavender, violet, dark blue. It got dark. We talked. I told her about seeing the woman at the house in Beverly Hills, and thinking it was her. I described the whole scene. Barbara laughed. She said suddenly: 'I lied.'

'About Hawaii? Forget it.'

'About that guy I told you about. The one who killed himself.'

I presumed she was about to tell me that the whole story was a fantasy. Instead, she said, 'It was me. There was no other girl. It was me he asked to sleep with his friends. And I did. I liked it.'

And she'd seen him walk from a window twenty-six floors up?

She kissed me and stood. Sand squeezed between her toes. She took pins from the back of her head and shook loose her hair. She peeled off her T-shirt, revealing tanned breasts and erect nipples. She stood over me.

Barbara said, 'I am the wind, I am the sea. Fuck me. Eat me, now.'

I looked around the beach. There was no one in sight. 'Here?'
She said, '*Eat me*, NOW.'
I did. Who was I to deny Barbara her wishes?

IT HAPPENED
ONE NIGHT

WE ARRIVED AT the Palamino Club at nine o'clock. The Palamino was in North Hollywood and a sign above the parking lot flashed red and blue neon: 'The King Lives . . . Tonite . . . The King Lives'. Moss had his hair slicked back. He wore a pink zoot suit. The jacket came to his knees and the trousers stopped two inches above patent pink alligator shoes. He said, 'I look like a prophylactic.'

Moss was getting these strange jobs. He had been hired to play rhythm guitar for a singer called Dwight Wonder who impersonated Elvis Presley, circa 1969, Las Vegas comeback period. Moss said, 'This guy's got it down tight. Leather suits. Sequinned suits. Mutton-chop sideburns and a diamond ring on his pinkie. He keeps going to the front of the stage to kiss women. He does a 22-minute version of "Suspicious Minds" and drinks Gatorade by the quart.'

Barbara asked how many cheeseburgers he ate.

I asked: 'Dwight *Wonder*?'

By nine-thirty the club was packed. There was no smoke at all in the low-ceilinged room. Moss said that people no longer smoked in Los Angeles. Everyone was too concerned about their health. There was even talk of *banning* the habit in Beverly Hills. Smokers would be fined, or have their Bullocks charge cards confiscated. 'Just look at this audience,' said Moss. 'Can't you smell the money? The San Fernando Valley. Another hour and they'll get steamed up, start swatting each other with their jewellery.'

We had a drink at the bar, and five minutes later Moss headed backstage, a pink exclamation mark pushing through the crowd.

Barbara said, 'Maybe I'll buy you a suit like that. You'd look kinda cute in pink.'

I groaned.

Barbara had ideas about my wardrobe. These ideas featured pointy boots, string ties and big cowboy hats. That wasn't so bad. They also featured headbands, wristbands, cycling shorts, tight-fitting bikini briefs emblazoned with slogans like 'Easy Rider' and 'Medium Rare', and a pair of expensive silver training shoes which were padded and cushioned and resembled the footwear the astronauts used for trudging about on the moon. 'They're very nice,' I said. 'But what am I supposed to *do* with them?' I had never owned a pair of training shoes in my life.

We had been living together for three weeks. Barbara had been working in the evening, I worked during the day. We fucked late at night and early morning. At the weekend, when not rethinking my appearance, we pushed a trolley up the aisles at Ralph's, went to the beach, and watched movies on TV. Barbara was happy. She told me so. She talked about trying to get a part in a movie.

Barbara and I found seats at a table. Two women were there already: blonde, sequinned, tanned, with pale blue eyes. They were like dolls. 'We're mother and daughter,' said one. 'But which is which?'

I stared. They were indistinguishable. I said, 'You must be twins.'

She laughed, a thin, nervous sound, and said, 'I'm the mother. And you're a true gentleman. I'm Lauren, and this is my daughter Kismet. Are you from New Zealand?'

'England.'

'New Zealand, England, Canada. I get my continents messed around.'

'I dig Australians,' said Kismet. 'They're cute. I dated this guy last year. He was Australian. He wore a hat just like Davy Crockett. He bought me a shirt that was so neat.'

'Are you here vacationing?'

'I'm working.'

'What kind of work do you do?'

'I clean swimming pools.'

'Oh,' she said, and asked what car I drove.

'I don't have one.'

'It's in the shop?'

'I don't drive.'

This woke Kismet from her reverie about Australians in outlandish headgear. She said, 'How do you get around? I mean, how do you get places?'

'I take the bus.'

'The bus? I've never been on the bus. Where do they go?'

'They go all over, baby,' said Lauren. 'The drivers take cocaine.'

'They do *what*?' I said.

'They freebase cocaine and they crash the buses.'

'Wow,' said Kismet. That seemed to sum it up.

'How do you know this?'

'Perhaps *I* should take the bus,' said Kismet.

'There was a story in the *Herald* only the other day. A driver smashed down a post in Century City, killed three people. The tests were positive.'

'Jesus,' I said. I remembered coming down from Hollywood a few nights before. The driver had taken the curves on Sunset at terrible speed, menacing with raised fist any passenger who dared to complain.

'Do you think,' said Kismet, 'that they have buses in Australia?'

Lauren and Barbara were already talking about something else. They had discovered common ground. 'You're putting me on,' said Barbara.

'Playmate of the Month, September 1964. Hef bought me a car, the cutest little Italian sports car.'

'What colour was it?'

'Red. I was eighteen. That was in Chicago. Then I was the Max Factor Girl, on the cover of lots of magazines. I moved to the coast. And I met this guy. The worst guy I ever met.'

'What did he do?'

'Took some pictures, kinda nasty pictures, you know the kind of thing I mean, with *animals*, and they were printed in one of those underground magazines. He sent a copy to Max Factor and that was the end of my contract. He thought it was a big joke.'

'That sucks,' said Barbara.

'The Sixties were real kind to me. I shot him with a .38. They gave me two years.'

'They put you in prison?'

'I didn't even kill the guy,' said Lauren.

At ten o'clock the band came on. Moss stood backstage, adjusting the guitar strap on his shoulder, looking awkward and gazing down at his pink alligator shoes. Dwight Wonder came to the front. He wore a suit which glittered and hugged his body. His chest was exposed. He swivelled his hips and aimed his mouth at the microphone: '*My hands are shakin' and my knees are weak, I can't seem to stand on my own two feet.*' He was about five feet tall, and fat, a dwarf Elvis who resembled the Michelin Man.

Lauren was in tears. 'I know it's true,' she said, 'but I just can't believe he's dead.'

I went to get drinks. I had to queue for a few minutes. A man was there, martini in hand. He said, 'Isn't this grotesque? My mind doesn't want to accept what my eyes are seeing. But then gin always makes me intellectual.'

'I know the guitar player.'

'The one with the suit? And those shoes?'

'That's him.'

'At least he looks embarrassed,' he said. He drained his martini and wiped his lips with his forefinger. 'I'm Drax. That's short for Dietrich Buchster Haader der Junger. D-R-A-X.'

'Like the James Bond villain?'

'I copyrighted the name. And you?'

'Richard,' I said.

'May I ask you something? Do you enjoy TV commercials?'

'Some.'

'I am an artist of the TV commercial. I used to make lots. That was in Eugene, Oregon. The station was bought by the Mafia. These guys came in from New York. They all wore overcoats and were called Morty. I guess it must have been the *Jewish* Mafia. I figured it was time to bale out.'

Drax was in his thirties. He had ginger hair and a moustache which he kept stroking. His speech was fast, nervous. He was in constant fear of interruption. When the Mafia had moved in on Oregon he had come to Los Angeles, hoping to make it as a film producer. He was in negotiation with Colonel Tom Parker for the rights to his life story, and was at the Palamino Club to check out Dwight Wonder as a possibility to play the great discovery of Parker's career, the young Elvis Presley. 'Wasted journey,' he said. 'Guy sounds good but looks like the pits. So fat. Nasty.'

He asked if I was on my own. I pointed to the table where Barbara sat with Lauren and Kismet. He bought three bottles of California champagne. We took them over. 'Hi,' he said. 'Hi. Hi. Hi. I'm Dietrich Buchster Haader der Junger.'

'Say again?' said Barbara.

'Drax for short.'

She shrugged. 'Right.'

I popped the champagne and poured.

'What are we celebrating?' said Lauren.

'I was about to tell Richard about my marriage.'

'You got married?' said Lauren.

'I got *divorced*. I was very unfair to my wife. Tried to control everything she did. What she ate. What clothes she bought. I liked to tie her up in the morning, before I went to work. With dental floss. She left me. I had a breakdown, but everything's OK now.'

At ten-fifteen Dwight Wonder, Moss and the rest of the band

were grinding through 'Return to Sender'. Drax said, 'I never liked that song.'

'I *love* Elvis,' said Lauren, giving him a stern look.

'Me too,' said Drax. 'I got all the records, all the movies on VCR.'

'What's your favourite?'

' "Roustabout".'

'You know,' said Lauren. 'When I was fifteen years old I used to dress like Barbara Stanwyck in that movie.'

'With the white angora sweater?'

'Right, that's right.'

Drax said, 'That's funny. So did I.'

Barbara asked about putting on women's clothes. Had I ever done it? If I could choose who to be like, who would it be? Molly Ringwald? Jackie Onassis? Joan Collins in *Dynasty*? Or maybe even Margaret Thatcher?

Was she serious?

Drax said to Lauren: 'May I ask you something?'

'Go right ahead?'

'Forgive me for asking, wine always makes me physical, but do *you* like to use dental floss?'

'Use dental floss for what?'

'For your teeth. Or other things. Whatever.'

Lauren said: 'Waxed or unwaxed?'

He smiled, and poured more champagne. He thanked me for introducing him to one of the more psychically aware women in Los Angeles. Kismet made a face. She seemed to dislike Drax. Perhaps it was because he wasn't Australian.

The show finished at twenty past eleven, after a version of 'Suspicious Minds' that lasted nineteen minutes (I timed it). Drax gave me a business card and told me to keep in touch. He went off with Lauren and Kismet, presumably to buy dental floss. Barbara and I waited for Moss, who arrived sweating and breathless. He suggested we go to a party in Pacific Palisades, where he'd heard various music-industry types were going to be.

The house was a steel and glass box, high on Entrada Drive, off Chautauqua Boulevard, and clung to the side of a canyon. It seemed insanely precarious. Moss said the houses here were in constant danger from mudslides. They could be swept away in moments. Living here was living on the edge, and being seen to do so. It was a display of the fact that the owner wasn't scared to take the chance. He said his family had once lived close by. His father had made a small fortune in the avocado business. He bought a yacht, a house, and a green Rolls-Royce. It matched the colour of the fruit. 'House came down one night after a storm,' Moss said. 'My dad never did anything that lasted. But when he lived, he lived.'

The garden smelled of pine needles. A blue shield said 'Protected by the Bel Air Patrol' and on the lawn a woman mimed peeling a banana. She was anorexically thin, and naked. 'Is this where the party's at?' said Moss. The woman didn't reply. She bit down on the imaginary fruit, and chewed.

'Lunchbox,' said Barbara.

A Mexican servant was at the door with glasses of white wine on a tray. Moss said he realized it was going to be the sort of Los Angeles party where no one drank a lot, no one took drugs, no one talked about sex and everyone hoped someone important was about to arrive.

'The lunchbox with the banana?' said Barbara.

Dwight Wonder was there, with his back to a curved window that overlooked the canyon. The lights of other houses were suspended in the darkness like lanterns. Dwight Wonder was with a man who wore a silk suit that sparkled. The man was saying that most people presumed Elvis Presley died on 16 August 1977, and most people presumed wrong. In fact he was still alive, on an island off the coast of Mexico. Priscilla went to see him once a month. This was gospel. He had it from someone at Lorimar. Moreover, Elvis was a man transformed: no more burgers, ice cream or Hershey bars. He was into health foods.

'Like bean sprouts and alfalfa?' asked Dwight Wonder.

The man in the suit continued: 'I could sell this to the *Enquirer* for $250,000. Don't tell me it doesn't beat some story about how a former Charley's Angel has suspected cancer of the cunt. But, Elvis. I mean to say, *Elvis*. You know how it is?'

'I know how it is,' said Dwight Wonder, all sympathy. He saw Moss and shouted, 'Yo, Moss. Come on over. I've got some news. Someone I want you to meet.'

I went to a table where another butler was fixing drinks. I got a scotch for me, bourbon and water for Barbara. She was wearing a blue dress and looked beautiful. There was still something about being with her: it left me breathless. A man in a red satin jogging suit had come up and was talking to her.

'The basic premise,' said the man in the satin jogging suit, 'is that the United States has been taken over by Canada.'

'By *Canada*?' said Barbara.

'Is that a realistic basis for a mini-series?'

'I wouldn't buy it.'

'That's what I told Lieberson.'

'You know the origin of the word Canada?' I said. 'Comes from the Spanish *que nada*. Means 'this is nothing'. *Que nada*, Canada.'

'Let me get a handle on this,' said Barbara. 'So Canada means . . . *nothing*?'

'That's it.'

The man pounced: '*That's* what I told Lieberson.' He turned away.

Barbara said, 'Guy came into the club the other day. A director. He asked me to audition for a part. Said I should learn a speech, something from a play or movie, something I choose myself. Will you help me?'

'Of course,' I said. I'd told Barbara that at college a friend and I used to learn dialogue from movies. The friend was a Welshman named Pete Davies. He was a literature student. In fact he read little apart from comic books which depicted muscular British marines singlehandedly smashing entire regiments of the Wehrmacht and Waffen SS. Davies, a.k.a. Cymru Clint, a.k.a. The Portmadoc Cowboy, a.k.a. War Mag Pete, was a great fantasist. He admired the clipped prose of James M. Cain and once began an essay on The Roman Plays with the sentences: 'Antony was a man who knew what he wanted. And knew how to get it. And what he wanted now was the voluptuous Egyptian bitch.' He was outraged when this did not win him the plaudits he expected. He enquired whether his tutor had ever read the opening of *The Postman Always Rings Twice*. Davies and I used to talk about the screen performances we most admired: Nicholson in *Chinatown*, Welles in *Touch of Evil*, Walbrook in *The Red Shoes*, Seberg in *Lilith*, Mitchum in *Thunder Road*, Eastwood in *High Plains Drifter* (Eastwood: 'Paint the town red.' Priest: 'You don't mean the church.' Eastwood: 'I mean . . . *especially* the church.'), and Alec Guinness as Bishop D'Ascoyne in *Kind Hearts and Coronets* ('I always say my west window has all the exuberance of Chaucer without, happily, any of the concomitant crudity of the period.'). We talked about this stuff each day, and left with third-class degrees.

'You don't seem to know about much . . .' said Barbara.

I didn't?

'. . . but I guess I'll have to trust you about this.'

I looked at my watch. It was nearly one in the morning. The party didn't seem like it was ever going to pick up. As the man with the satin jogging suit came up again to confer with Barbara, I moved to a corner of the room where there was a woman with black hair like Brooke Shields. She wore chunky ear-rings which had probably been looted from an Aztec temple. She seemed uninterested in the proceedings and gave me a stare that said: *what can you do for my career?*

'I can do great things for your career.' I said.

'Have you seen Johnny?' she said.

I told her I'd never heard of Johnny.

She said Johnny was the host. Johnny was a cool customer. Sometimes he gave parties and didn't show up. He watched the whole thing on video later. Her eyes gestured towards the ceiling where a camera filmed the proceedings. 'Are you in pictures?'

'I wrote a screenplay once. In England. That's where I come from. I'm working on some ideas now.'

She didn't seem interested, so I told her the joke about the Polish actress who tried to break into pictures by sleeping with the writer ('Except at home we'd call her an *Irish* actress,' I said), then the one about my grandmother being eighty-seven and not needing glasses, she just drinks from the bottle.

She said, 'What precisely, can you do for my career?'

'Nothing, as such.'

'I think I should call security. I think I should definitely call security.'

The man in satin came up. He said, 'That story you told me about Canada. Is it true?'

'I *think* so,' I said.

'Guy over there said it was horseshit. Said "Canada" meant something different altogether.'

'Perhaps I heard it somewhere. It could be a lie.'

'A *lie?*'

Moss came up. He seemed desperate. He said that someone at the party was talking about giving Dwight Wonder a $1.5m record contract. This made him angry. He said, 'I've got a .38 in the car. How would it be if I blasted Dwight and told Mr EMI to go get himself a new Elvis, this one leaks?'

I said, 'I don't think that would be a good idea.' Moss carried a gun in his car?

Barbara came up. She said, 'What's the problem here?'

The satin man said, 'You're a very sick individual. You know that? A very sick individual.'

The woman who was like Brooke Shields said, 'You mean there's someone over there who's going to be someone?'

Moss said, 'Let's go to Las Vegas.'

It was one-fifteen. Moss drove a 1971 Cadillac de Ville, a dark blue convertible, long and low, a gas guzzler with flaking chrome and a leaky top. Oily puddles slopped on the floorboards and vicious mosquitoes lived in empty beer cans on the back seat. We headed east through the Palisades on a dark and winding stretch of Sunset. The engine made ominous *clunketa-clunketa* noises.

Moss said, 'Guy who sold me this car was a Mormon. He had false teeth and a $500 suit. Guys like that they see guys like me coming, they look around the lot and say, "Hey, Dutch, remember that Caddy, the one Mrs Glucksman brought in the other day, the one with the sugar in the tank and the totally *wrecked* oil sump? Bring it on out, I think we've got a customer." And I get eaten alive. Every car I ever bought turned to shit.'

Thirty minutes later we stopped at the Bob's Big Boy on Montana Avenue. The five-foot-high statue of Bob – a grinning child in red and white check trousers – was outside as usual, except that someone had sawn off the statue's head and the burger he held invitingly on his upturned palm and switched the two, so the severed head was on the hand and the burger on the neck. It was probably part of a campaign against the Bob's Big Boy chain. I'd read about it. A statue of Bob had been found in cement at the end of the pier at Huntington Beach. The previous week another had been kidnapped in Culver City. A ransom note was received and after two days the statue was found, in a canyon off Mulholland Drive, blindfolded and with a gunshot wound to the head. The film director David Lynch had started a counter-campaign: 'Save Our City, Save Big Bob'.

Moss said, 'I once had lunch every day for a year at the same Bob's Big Boy. That was up in the valley. I was working with my father at the time, training attack dogs.'

'Training *attack* dogs?'

'Dobermans, Rottweilers, German shepherds. Our speciality was mastiffs. Real mean dogs.'

'What kind of people buy attack dogs?'

'Rich people. Scared people. Psycho people. People who live at Venice Beach,' he said.

The Bob's Big Boy was deserted. The waitress laughed at Moss's pink suit and took our order. She sat down at the table. 'I've been working six hours already tonight,' she said. 'I'm bored.' Her name was Tracia. She was eighteen, she said, and she was only working here until her boyfriend sent her the money to travel to Europe. Her boyfriend was Dutch, a clog manufacturer.

She said, 'We only met for one hour on a plane. Since then we've spoken to each other on the phone every day. Doesn't that sound romantic?'

Highly improbable was what it sounded, said Barbara.

Tracia was in a dream. She said, 'When I get there, I think I'm gonna be a painter, like Vincent van Gogh.'

By two-thirty we were back on the road, heading east on the Santa Monica freeway, and a K-SURF news bulletin said how a group of surfers had paddled out into the ocean, waiting for an enormous tidal wave to come in from Hawaii. They thought an earthquake was about to cause the end of the world. I wondered if Norris was out there, bobbing up and down, hoping for the ride of his life.

Moss was more cheerful. He said that his father had actually wanted him to become a musician. He taught Moss to play the piano, but died off Catalina Island when his yacht capsized in a freak squall, leaving debts so bad Moss had to give up his studies and take a job to help support his mother and sister. Moss had worked selling insurance and when the debt was cleared went back to music. 'Another year and I know I'll make it,' he said. 'I've just got to get through the next year.'

Maybe he would make it. Since I'd been in Los Angeles I'd heard all these stories. Making it: it could take a lifetime, it might never happen and occasionally the process did occur overnight. Stories in the last category were absorbed into the city's mythology. They became part of the fabric, sometimes literally. Barbara had told me the story of a UCLA graduate she knew who sold a script called 'Lethal Weapon' to Warner Bros for $1.5m plus a percentage. His name was Shane Black. He was twenty-two. Before the movie was released, before it was even cast, Barbara began to see strange graffiti on the walls of women's restrooms in all the bars along Pico and Westwood Boulevards: 'Shane Black *is* a Lethal Weapon'; 'Shane, Weapon, Lethal'; 'Shane – Check *that* Weapon' etc. 'I know one bimbo, creams her jeans at the mention of his name,' Barbara said. Success, it seemed, had usurped the qualities of glamour, excitement, even orgasm, that once belonged to sex. 'Imagine getting a $1.5m contract,' said Barbara. 'It would be like coming for a year.'

Moss drove at reckless speed, as if trying to make up for lost time. It was five-thirty, and Barbara was asleep in the back, waking occasionally to slap at a mosquito, and I saw a red glimmer above the desert. Moss said, 'That's it. Las Vegas. The butt end of the American dream. The only town where I ever saw false teeth in a pawn shop window. And prosthetic devices. I've seen a guy trade his glass eye for one more roll.'

Another thirty minutes and dawn was breaking. I could make out details in the desert: cactus plants and sage brush, debris littering the sand, rock eroded into weird and tortured shapes. As it grew light the rock changed colour, from purple to blue, and then to red. We passed a scrapyard that was over a mile long and may have contained a million disintegrating wrecks. In a gully at the side of the interstate a man leaned over the open door of his truck, aiming a rifle at a tyre. Smoke puffed from the barrel and the tyre bobbled among the rocks. An echoing crack, the shot, came a moment later. Moss said, 'Every now and then one of those guys will turn around and take a bead as you go past. Maybe only for a few seconds, but it puts you real uptight.'

Soon after we shot over the crest of a hill and there was Las Vegas, a suburban sprawl with a congregation of high-rise buildings at its centre. These were the big hotels and their neon lights were still on, bleeding light into the morning. Moss said, 'If it turns out Hell has been designed by the New York mob, it will be a lot like Las Vegas.'

At six-twenty Las Vegas seemed ghostly, unreal. Las Vegas Boulevard, the Strip, was deserted, strewn with litter and on either side the big hotels seemed cheated by the day, as if made of cardboard. Caesar's Palace resembled a façade for a multi-storey car park. At this hour of the morning Las Vegas was not impressive.

Moss pulled up outside the Flamingo Hilton. The Flamingo had pink windows and a limousine outside which once belonged to Al Capone. The limousine was long and grey, heavy with armour plating. Barbara and I got out, and Moss gunned the Cadillac down the Strip.

'Where did Moss go?' said Barbara, yawning.

'Some club outside town.'

'He's gonna play there sometime?'

'I'm not sure. He wanted to meet someone.'

'Let's get some coffee.'

It was six twenty-three when we met the first man. He lurched towards us on the pavement. He was in bad shape, tall and scraggy, with a filthy, torn suit. He carried a copy of the *Las Vegas News* in one hand and in the other held a bottle of Pepto-Bismol from which he took long, gulping swigs. He seemed unhinged. 'Seven, nine, *craps*,' he babbled, 'seven, eleven, *snake-eyes*.'

'Are you OK?' I asked.

'Just tell me,' he said. 'Just say the word and I'll blow my brains out.'

'Don't do it,' said Barbara.

The man thought for a moment. 'No?'

'Really, no.'

The man lifted the bottle of pink liquid to his lips. 'You know something, lady, you're right. I've got to get right back in there. Just guts it out,' he said. 'Could you find it in your heart to lend me, say, $2,500?'

Five minutes later we met the second man. We had just walked past a metal pole, on top of which rotated an enormous silver shoe. That man had a red face and black hair like a Beatle wig. Fat wrinkled over his collar. I asked if he knew anywhere that was open for breakfast.

'You want coffee?' His accent was thick and clumsy.

'And something to eat.'

'I am Horst. I make you breakfast,' he said.

I said we didn't want to put him to any trouble. He was insistent. He took my arm and led us to a building set back from the road. From the outside it resembled a large, pink dog kennel. That was how it seemed on the inside as well. There was a smell of urine and an Afghan burped and farted in a basket in one corner of the room.

'This is Dirty Harry,' said Horst. 'He is very old now, very fat. He makes urine all the time on the floor. This is why there is the smell.' A fierce belch confirmed Dirty Harry's presence.

Horst plugged in an electric kettle for coffee. He pushed slices of bread into a toaster. He explained that he had lived in Las Vegas since 1971. He was Norwegian. He had grown up in Oslo, and came to America when his father's lumber business went bankrupt. He had lived for six months in Boston, then moved to Las Vegas. He said, 'You from England, no?'

'That's right.'

'I was there in England, in the war. Now I make study of the writing of Graham Greene.'

'I saw him once.'

'You did,' said Horst, delighted by the revelation. He laughed, and fat shook round his neck like a noose. 'You saw Graham Greene? Where?'

'In London. He was going into a Catholic church. The one mentioned in *The End of the Affair*.'

'This is my favourite book. About faith and fidelity. So tortured,' he said. 'And Mr Greene. What was he like?'

'Very tall.'

'I see. I see.' He scratched his chin with plump fingers and turned to Barbara. 'You and him,' he said. 'You wish to become man and wife?'

I considered this a strange twist in the conversation, even if we had just been discussing Graham Greene.

'You are here after all,' he said. 'In The Hitching Post wedding chapel.' I looked around. There was a cross on the wall, a bible on a chair, boxes of confetti on a shelf. It was discreet. The place didn't *look* like a wedding chapel.

Barbara made up her mind in a few seconds. She said, 'Let's do it.'

'Just like that?'

'Why not?'

'You really think so?'

'We had to meet for a reason, right?'

At six thirty-five Horst sold us the ring, for $19.50. It was just like 22 carat, he said, no one would ever notice the difference, we could give it to our grandchildren. We drank our coffee and went with him to the Clark County Court to pick up the marriage licence. That took less than fifteen minutes. Then we were back at The Hitching Post. Dirty Harry was awake, howling, Horst threw fistfuls of confetti in the air, and I pushed the ring on Barbara's finger. At four minutes to seven we became man and wife.

I lay on a king-size bed in a $25 room at the Circus Circus casino. Barbara was asleep beside me, clutching a pillow like it was a teddy bear. I remembered that before I'd left London I'd been to see Heywood. I'd known Heywood for years. I told him I'd had a heart attack. He was a consultant at the Middlesex Hospital and expert in the output of the Rolling Stones, 1963–1971. He once gave me a black ink drawing of Keith Richards, looking gaunt and devastated. Heywood was an avid Keith Richards man. 'Mick's all right,' he said. 'Mick isn't bad. But Keith *is* the Rolling Stones.' Heywood claimed to have performed major chest surgery while listening to 'Nineteenth Nervous Breakdown'. On that day he wore a white coat and a red tie crusted with egg yolk. I explained I'd been watching Errol Flynn in *The Sea Hawk* on TV; a terrible pain had scorched my chest; I knew I was about to die. He smiled. I said I was serious. He shrugged and led me to a nurse who shot X-rays of my chest and back, and then into a grey and sour-smelling examination room. Paint flaked from the walls. He put a stethoscope to my heart, checked my pulse and blood pressure, took my temperature. He inspected the X-rays and said there was nothing wrong with me that he could see. I definitely hadn't had a heart attack. He really couldn't say what had happened: medicine was such an imprecise science.

'How's Jane?' he asked, lighting a Marlboro. 'How are you two getting on?'

'OK. Not too good.'

'Why's that?'

I'd told him that I was, well, bored.

I got off the bed and went to the window. Signs twirled above The Strip: 'Graveyard Keno is back', 'Slots Hysteria', 'Girls . . . girls . . . girls in pornographic shoes'. I was in Las Vegas. I had married Bunny Barbara. Bored? I'd licked that problem alright.

At noon Barbara and I went out. We had our arms round each other. In the lift a balding man said: 'I was married one time. That was when I was in the demolition business. Three weeks later I fell through the roof of a building we were knocking down, thirty-five feet, broke my arms and legs, had terrible internal injuries. My wife was already pregnant. She went to work in a department store, divorced me while I was still in traction. Yessir, marriage is a noble institution.' When he got out of the lift Barbara and I looked at each other, and giggled.

We walked up The Strip, through the air-conditioned lounges of the Flamingo, past the rows of video poker games and churning slot machines, and out into the garden. There was a plaque in honour of Bugsy Siegel, the New York gangster who saw the Nevada desert and decided to put the Flamingo, the first of the big gambling hotels, there. The plaque was bronze and surrounded by tall rose bushes flowering pink and red. It said:

Remember Filthy Frankie Giannattsio? How about notorious Big Howie Dennis? Perhaps you recall the scurrilous Mad Dog Neville. They were all associated with Bugsy at one time or another and coincidentally they all vanished into thin air rather suddenly. No trace was ever found of them. The rumour has it that if you stand on this spot at midnight under a full moon you can hear three muffled voices saying, 'Bugsy, how do you like the roses, Bugsy?'

Barbara said Patterson had once written a gangster-script. It was called 'Born to Shoot'. She said he had developed a psychic relationship with the character. They used to talk to each other. I wondered if by any chance the gangster had run into Barbara's father, somewhere up there on the astral plane. Barbara said, 'Guy told Patterson to go out kill someone, so he could write about it. Patterson didn't do it, of course. He just bought a pistol and joined a gun club. Kinda neat, huh?'

I said I thought it was a very good thing she wasn't living with Patterson any more.

Moss arrived. He was sweating, and his pink suit was scarred with oil. He had the air of George Custer at Little Big Horn. He said, 'I had to wait an hour before the guy I was supposed to deal with showed up. When the guy did arrive he was as big as a garbage truck. The first thing he did was to offer to remove my lungs, because he thought I was someone else. I got that straightened out. Then I was coming back into town and the fuel pump on the Caddy died. I had to wait two hours for the repair.'

He sighed and forced a smile. 'Tell me,' he said, 'how did you two spend your morning?'

PART
—4—

FALLING APART

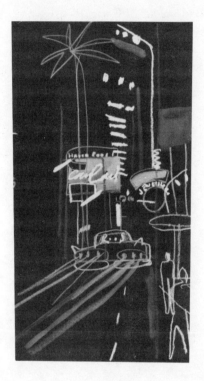

IN MY DREAM I wore the bunny suit, and walked in stilettos along a corridor. A door opened into what seemed to be a hospital operating theatre. There were oxygen tanks and machines with lights and dials. Surgical instruments gleamed on a table. Barbara and Patterson were in conversation, laughing. When he saw me, Patterson stopped laughing and forced his expression into one of profound sensitivity. He took me by the hand. 'This is the best thing all round,' he said.

'Really,' said Barbara.

'The only way,' said Patterson, 'the best solution.'

'Really,' said Barbara, giggling.

A tall man came in. He wore a surgeon's gown and a mask covered the lower half of his face. 'I am Dr Garcia,' he said. 'I am here to help you. To help you realign. And harmonize.' He bent over the table and picked up a scalpel. He advanced towards me, his wide jaw set in a grin. The scalpel carved open the stretched material of the bunny suit and Dr Garcia scrutinized what lay beneath. 'Yup, just as I thought,' he said, and seized my penis between thumb and forefinger. 'We're gonna have to do something about *this*.'

I woke up. A radio was blaring. I was at the beach with Barbara. The beach was like the beach always was: people shouting, men like Charles Atlas plunging through the surf on bodyboards, women with swimsuits and suntans and bodies it was painful to look at. I hadn't told Barbara but I didn't like the beach. It was the physical perfection. It was Los Angeles, I had decided, not Hitler's Germany, which had given the world a master race. I was developing the theory. Throughout the 1920s and 1930s the strongest, fittest and most beautiful people came by the thousand to the city, hoping to make it in the movies. Only a few succeeded but most stayed on anyway, enjoying the climate, getting healthy on the diet, marrying each other, *interbreeding*, having children who had children who looked like these people here on the beach: lean, tanned, blond, strong – bikini storm-troopers, surf Nazis. I was convinced. I was certain that one would come up and boot sand in my face.

The sun was relentless. My sunglasses were on and my shoulders were toasting. I needed an oxygen tent. Barbara and I had been preparing for her audition. A thick paperback titled *1001 Movie Speeches for Actors* lay beside me on the towel. We'd argued over what lines she should prepare, settling for something of Jane Fonda's from *Klute*. The thing about going to the beach with Barbara was that someone always tried to take her home. Men in gold swimming costumes offered her rides in their Ferraris. Photographers suggested she come and pose for an hour or two at their Malibu studios. Sometimes it started innocently. At the moment, for instance, she was at the ocean's edge, about to race with one of the lifeguards. This happened regularly. Barbara was the sprint champion of Santa Monica beach. The lifeguard's name was Tom. He was a big factor in the surf Nazi theory. He had a blond crew cut and very wide, bronzed shoulders. Each of his fists was roughly the same size as his head. A distance had been measured out for the race and a crowd had gathered to watch. Barbara dropped into a sprinter's crouch, wrists arched, left knee poised inches above the sand. Someone flagged a T-shirt and the race began. Tom the lifeguard went into an early lead.

'Roberto,' a voice said loudly. It belonged to a woman. She was tall and tanned in a ketchup-red swimsuit. On her thigh was a white scar in the shape of a figure eight.

'Roberto,' she said again. I looked around. She seemed to be talking to me.

'Excuse me,' I said. 'Do I know you?'

She gave me a tolerant smile. She told me we had met at a party the previous week. Didn't I remember? It was in a warehouse downtown, that place with old rock videos and bats flying in the rafters. 'John Gregory was there and Carlos, and Millie did the trick with the peach,' she said.

'I don't think so.'

'Definitely. I remember. Millie definitely did the trick with the peach.'

'I mean I don't remember us having met. I wasn't at the party.'

'You *weren't*? Your name *is* Roberto?'

I said it was Richard, actually. I wondered about the trick with the peach.

'How totally weird,' she said. 'How totally, totally weird. But you are English, right?'

I confirmed this. She held her head on one side and squinted at me. She grinned, revealing pointy teeth and gums which matched the colour of her swimsuit. It was a predatory mouth. I guessed her age at about thirty. She said, 'Then you must help me with something.'

'I must?'

'Of course. Don't go away now.'

I told her I wasn't going anywhere, and she trotted off. I looked towards the ocean. The race had reached halfway. Barbara was making her move. She stretched out, legs pumping, and went past the lifeguard as though he were immobile.

The woman came back, with a hefty book. She said, 'I need some help with a London accent.'

'I don't understand.'

'I'm studying for a role.'

'What sort of London accent?'

'You mean there's more than one?'

'Quite a few.'

'You see. I really do need the advice. It's just so important to get these things right,' she said. She dropped beside me on the towel and handed me the book. It was a volume from the collected works of George Bernard Shaw. The black and yellow cover was greasy with a suntan oil that smelled of coconuts. She wanted to know all about Eliza Doolittle. What part of London did she live in? What was the house like? What would her family do for entertainment? Would they have entertainment at all? What was her *total* lifestyle? And how did she speak? That seemed most important of all. The woman wanted to know, precisely.

I looked at her. She was expectant. She was so close I could smell her breath: white wine and apricots. Was she serious, or was this an elaborate pick-up? Perhaps she came to the beach with an entire library to cover all possible encounters: a German would be given Buchner, or Goethe perhaps; a Norwegian would be greeted with Ibsen; a Frenchman, Racine; a Greek, Sophocles; and so on. I wondered about Australians. Had Patrick White written any plays?

Or perhaps she was crazy, a real psycho, a member of the surf-Nazi Gestapo. I grimly imagined a house converted to a torture chamber, each room decked out with instruments for the administration of pain. I looked for Barbara. She had won the race and was chaired aloft by hulking beach boys. They carried her away, roaring. I looked at the woman. Her eyes were fixed on mine, waiting. I told myself I was being paranoid. I tried to remember what I knew about *Pygmalion*. It was very little.

I said, 'It's a long time since I read the play.'

'Anything will be useful. Anything at all.'

'She grew up in the East End of London, probably in a small terraced house with an outside toilet.'

'They had to go outside to the john?'

'It wasn't unusual in those days. It must have been the same here.'

'I wasn't around then,' she said.

'Anyway, Eliza lived in this house. She probably didn't go out much because she had to work all the time, and she sortuv 'ad a voice loik this. Are ew jokin? Cor, lumme, streuth, know what I mean?'

'A Cockney accent.'

'You know?'

She knew?

'Yeah, I know that stuff,' she said, flapping at an insect which buzzed round her head. 'Would you like to tie me up?'

'Excuse me?'

'Would you like to tie me up?' She smiled, revealing her terrible gums. 'Let's go to my apartment. Let's go right now. You can do anything you want to me.'

'I don't think so.'

'Anything at all, except fuck me.'

I said, 'I've got this theory. About California. It goes like this . . .'

'I mean it,' she said, 'I really mean it.'

'The movie industry got going in the 1920s. The strongest, fittest, most beautiful . . .'

'You don't think I'm attractive?' She frowned.

'You're very attractive.'

'Then what's the matter?'

I looked down. My toes wriggled on the towel. A light breeze rattled the pages of *1001 Movie Speeches for Actors*. I looked again towards the ocean. I'd lost sight of Barbara.

I said, 'I'm here with someone else.'

The woman leaned close. I felt her breath on my cheek. She said, 'Faggot.'

I said I rather thought I'd like to read the paper now and picked up the *LA Times*. I examined its pages with maniacal concentration. On page four there was a story headlined 'Gaol for Groucho'. It said: 'Allen Strick, 53, suspected of being one of two men who robbed 11 Los Angeles area banks, has been arrested at his Glendale home and booked on one charge of bank robbery, authorities said today. The bandits, who dressed as priests, construction workers, businessmen, Walt Disney characters and members of the Marx Bros comedy team, allegedly robbed the banks of $380,000 over a 2½-year period.' In Los Angeles even the bank robbers were taking auditions.

The woman's face was still close to mine. She said, 'Can I have my book, *faggot?*' I gave it to her, keeping my eyes fixed on the paper. I heard her move away across the sand. I lay back on the towel and closed my eyes, grinning with relief, thinking: *anything except fuck me?*

'Who was that?' said Barbara.

I blinked. I said, 'Some girl. An actress. She wanted advice about a London accent.'

'A London accent?'

'Crazy, isn't it? Perhaps I should start an acting studio. Me and Lee Strasberg.'

'Oh,' said Barbara. She fanned a wad of dollar bills. 'I won. Easy. Like taking candy from a baby.'

'I saw. How did Tom take it?' I said, and at that moment Tom came into view, marching towards us. His walk was a goosestep.

'Yo, Babs,' he called. 'I'll beat you one of these days.' His huge feet shuffled. His muscles trembled. His bullet head rocked and bobbed. It seemed impossible for him to keep still. 'Wanna give me another shot at the title?'

'Some time.'

'How about now?'

Barbara inspected the sky. A lone cloud was sidling towards the sun. She viewed this with disapproval. 'I think we'll leave the beach now,' she said.

Tom was shattered. He said, 'I'm bummed. I'm totally bummed.' He said it, he totally did.

'We have to take the bus.'

'The *bus*,' said Tom.

'My car's in the shop. Richard doesn't drive.'

The smile vanished from Tom's face and was replaced by an expression of complete bewilderment. He flicked beads of sweat from his forehead with a meaty finger. A balloon seemed to rise from his skull, with the message: *Does not drive?* A thought occurred to him and the smile returned. He said, 'Say, I could give you guys a ride. You could come back to my place.'

Barbara said, 'That's real nice of you.'

I said, 'But we couldn't possibly. Thanks for the offer.'

Tom said, 'Hey, guys. It'd be no trouble.'

'No, thanks.'

'Really?'

'We like to take the bus.'

'You do?'

'We *love* to take the bus.'

Tom found this incomprehensible. His mouth dropped open. 'I'm heavily bummed. But whatever you guys wanna do, I guess that's OK.' His bullet head bobbed, and pecked Barbara on the cheek. He grasped my hand and pumped it up and down. He said, 'Babs, I guess I'll see you around,' and ran towards the sea, legs ploughing the sand.

Barbara said, 'That was rude.'

'I don't think Tom minded.'

'Tom's a nice guy.'

I said, 'Tom was dropped on his head as a baby.'

She laughed, kissed me. 'What did she really want?'

'Who?'

'The woman, dummy.'

'She was trying to pick me up.'

Silence.

'It's true.'

Barbara gave me a disbelieving look.

'She wanted me to go to her apartment. She wanted me to tie her up.'

'With chains and handcuffs, I guess. Or silk ties.'

'She didn't specify.'

She said, 'Your imagination, your mind.'

I wondered what *that* was supposed to mean.

I walked with Barbara towards 4th St in Santa Monica. I thought about the bus in Los Angeles: it was the way to travel. Once I had waited for over two hours at the corner of Sunset and Crescent Hills Boulevard when a driver with a cowboy hat and a drawling voice like Harrison Ford decided he was sick of his job. His solution to the problem was to stop the bus and make everyone get off. We watched from the pavement as he made a sweeping turn, gunned the engine and headed back up Sunset, laughing and waving his hat. Behind me a woman in a pink shirt that hugged tight across her breasts said 'Ain't that a bitch', took out a bag of walnuts and smashed them in her palm, one by one. A thin, spotty man told his girlfriend how he made a TV commercial with Roy Orbison, 'You know, guy who did *Pretty Woman, pretty woman dada dada street*, from then on my career was downhill, I tell ya showbiz sucks, I've had it with showbiz, I've had it with the green tuna fish salad,' and a young Mexican with a dripping blood design on his T-shirt prowled up and down the shelter, staring with angry eyes. We had waited. And we had waited some more. By turn I felt pissed off, edgy, scared. Finally I was just bored. I no longer paid attention to the woman who cracked walnuts, the stalking Mexican, or even the drivers who went by in their cars with the windows open, shouting '*Lo-sers, asshole losers*'. Eventually another bus had come down the hill, burping fumes. We got on. There was a kid at the back, about twelve years old with ginger hair. He had a skateboard wedged between his feet and his smile was an ingratiating gleam. We were somewhere in Beverly Hills when the kid pulled out a tiny silver-handled automatic. It looked like a toy. He pressed it to the head of a man in a business suit and said so fast I nearly couldn't hear, 'Gimmeallyomoneyrightnowmotherfuckertherwiseblowyo-headfuckincleanoff.' The man had been so terrified he could scarcely put his hand in his jacket to reach for his wallet.

I told Barbara none of this. She had her blue-and-gold LA Rams bag over her shoulder and her bare legs were tucked into

Nike trainers. Her movements were all spring and grace. She said, 'You really like travelling on the bus?'

'It's democratic.'

She made a snorting sound. 'Does democracy arrive on time?'

'Never had to wait more than five minutes,' I lied, and when we were at the stop the Venice Boulevard bus, the 33, did pull up almost immediately. We got on and the bus moved forward, rattling and juddering. It was a very old bus. The smudgy pictures of missing children – Have you seen Maria? Disappeared 3-23-80, Aged 7; Have you seen Clarence? Last seen 6-25-78, Aged 14; Have you seen William? Last seen 9-1-82, Aged 4. Contact the Transit Police 213-800-8000 – were years out of date. A stained, tattered poster asked: 'Have You Been a Victim of a Transit Crime?', and the smoked Plexiglass windows were loose and flapped like insect wings. At the next stops more and more passengers trudged on board. Soon the bus was packed. A gang of bad boys came through the crowd, shoving and jostling, making for the back. One wore a blue Dodgers cap and one held a Mickey's Big Mouth in a brown paper bag. One carried a baseball bat and one had a knife tucked in his belt. All were drunk, or stoned, or both. Unease rippled along the bus.

I said, 'I think we're in trouble.'

One of the bad boys had stopped by our seat. It was the one in the Dodgers cap. A livid scar ran down his cheek. He appraised Barbara's legs and turned to his companions. He said, 'Check the chick. Look at those thighs. Like Bambi. Oh, man.'

I said, 'Watch out, you.'

He grabbed my arm: 'What the fuck did you say?'

It was a fair question. What *had* I said? And why had I said it? I thought: I am about to become a statistic on the Transit Crime Computer.

He said, 'Watch out. Watch *out*. What kind of weird shit is that? Where are you from, man? Venezuela?'

'He's from England,' said Barbara.

The bad boy ignored this. He put his arms on my shoulders and kissed me. He said, 'Go suck your tailpipe, nerdy. And keep out of my face.' He pushed his way to the back of the bus.

Barbara said, 'Nice move.'

I said, 'Another triumph for democracy.'

At the back the bad boys were shouting and laughing. The other passengers were being very English about the situation, ignoring the bad boys, pretending they were invisible, inaudible, but phrases loomed out: 'Fucking bitch . . . trash the guy . . . waste the sucker . . . roll the mother . . . get myself a piece . . . gut the turkey . . . pop the dude.' I presumed they were referring to me.

Barbara rubbed a sleeve against the grimy window. She said, 'I think we're on the wrong bus.'

I said, 'You're telling me.'

'I mean this bus isn't going the right way. We're on Lincoln. We shouldn't be on Lincoln. Should we?'

I looked out of the window. She was right. We were on Lincoln, heading in completely the wrong direction. The bus banked suddenly to the left, sweeping down the on-ramp of the Marina Freeway. The motion was so violent that an old couple were spilled into the aisle. They screamed. The bad boys at the back were also reacting. They were angry: 'Hey man . . . where are we? . . . this bus is on the frigging *freeway*, man . . . where the fuck is this bus going? . . . this ain't no fucking LA.'

A black woman was at the front, talking to the driver. She shouted that the driver had been driving this route for only two days. He didn't know his way around yet. He was lost.

'Whadidya say?' said one of the bad boys.

'The driver of the bus is lost. Does anyone know where we are?'

'Lost?'

'Oh, shit . . .'

'Believe it, man . . .'

'Oh . . . *shit.*'

The bad boy with the baseball bat stood up. He was tall and rangy, and smoked the biggest joint I've ever seen, a cigar-sized spliff that leaked marijuana on the floor. He swaggered down the aisle, saying 'Ladies and gentlemen. My name is Chokey. I am now taking control here.' He stood at the front, pointing the baseball bat, announcing that this RTD would now boldly go where no RTD had gone before. He accompanied his directions with an erratic commentary: 'On our left we see the wonderful Howard Hughes recreation centre, now we all know what a wild and crazy guy Howard was, and what sort of fun he was into, how he liked to design female underwear 'n' all, so I guess we're all just bustin' to break in there and get us some . . . *recreation*. A way over there to our right there's the MGM Studios where they make movies and *Dallas* and shit, and an airport where lots of small *aeroplanes* take off to buzz the jets coming out of LAX and no one does shit about it 'cos this is a free country, guy can fly his plane wherever the fuck he likes, and just here on the left, that's Washington High, where I used to know this chick, she was hot, and I'm sure you folks would love to hear about the stuff we used to do together, beat anything you can see on video, but I ain't telling . . .'

After fifteen minutes of this, he gave the bat a final waggle, and the bus was back on course, back on Venice. There were cheers. I pushed the bell-tape and we stood to get off.

'Nerdy wants off the bus,' said the one with the Dodgers cap. 'Nerdy don't dig the magical mystery tour. Nerdy wants to go back to Venezuela.'

The pneumatic doors hissed open. We got off. Barbara suggested that next time I might, possibly, consider accepting Tom's offer of a ride. I said, 'Next time.'

I called Takowsky. He was as suave as ever. I told him I'd been thinking, had lots of new ideas. Did he want to hear about them? He said of course he wanted to hear about them, but not now. He was pushed for time. He told me to make notes and send them in. I said that was fine, and perhaps he'd like to hear about just one of the ideas immediately. He chuckled. He said he'd like nothing better but he was on his way out to see his tailor about some new suits and he was in a blind rush to make it in time for lunch with a very famous client who he was taking to the only restaurant in the entire Los Angeles area which had three *unlisted* phone numbers. He said they cooked the most delicious rabbit there. They fattened the animals with foie-gras and slaughtered them on the premises. It was exquisite, he said.

Norris and I were up on Mulholland, a remote stretch near Stone Canyon. The van bounced and jolted. We'd gone too far. The road had turned into a dirt track. I told Norris we were lost. We stopped and got out to look at a map. At the roadside were purple flowers covered in dust. A twisted, rusting door lay at the bottom of a steep bank. Everything was silent. Below, a thin layer of smog was over the city like tissue paper. Norris said Mulholland Drive had these weird extremes: back in the direction from which we'd come were the spectacular houses where young movie czars lived; here it was like a desert. Mulholland was named after William Mulholland, an Irish immigrant who became chief engineer of the Los Angeles water department and one of the city's legendary robber barons. At the turn of the century he devised a system of aqueducts and channels to bring water from the Owens Valley, two hundred miles away, and allow Los Angeles to flourish in an inhospitable landscape. Farmers in Owens Valley went bankrupt while Mulholland built a dam at Santa Ana to collect the water he'd plundered. The dam collapsed about twenty years later, releasing a tidal wave which killed over four hundred. So Mulholland built another, pointed to the water it contained and said, 'There it is, *take it.*'

'Dude,' said Norris. 'The LA councillors liked that statement so much they named a street after him.'

I knew this story already. It had been used as a basis for the film *Chinatown*, and standing up there on Mulholland, I remembered a foggy night in Cambridge when I saw Jack Nicholson tell a shaggy dog story about the way Chinamen screw and follow Faye Dunaway's smashed tail-light, and I fell in love with Los Angeles. In the movie it was a city of blinding white by day, and velvety purples and blues by night. It seemed corrupt, exotic, dangerous.

Norris said, 'We'll have to go back.' We got in the van and turned round. Ten minutes later the road was tarmac again and soon we were in the territory of the big houses, lurking behind daunting walls and designer security. We found the one we were looking for, Norris held his ID in front of a video camera, a black iron gate slid open. We drove in. The house was a square box with white stucco walls and windows in smoked glass. It rose on stilts like a Bauhaus nightmare. We parked and walked down to the pool. There was no one around.

'Oh wow,' said Norris. 'Will you look at that?'

I did. And saw that the water in the pool was a deep red colour, like blood. I asked whether we shouldn't call the police. Norris poked a tentative finger, and sniffed: 'I don't *think* it's blood,' he said. He'd never seen anything like this, but he thought he had the answer. He went to the van and came back with a squat tub marked PurKlenz. Norris said, 'I put this stuff in a pool over in the Palisades one time, I thought there was gonna be an eruption. Started bubbling and frothing like Mount Fuji.' He stood on the diving board and dumped the tub's contents into the water.

The blue spread like thin fingers into the red and Norris grinned, saying 'Whaddya know? I think it's working,' but after two or three minutes the PurKlenz gave up the ghost and we watched, appalled, as the water turned an even deeper red, a hideous scarlet. 'Oh shit,' said Norris.

A woman came down the steps from the house. She wore sunglasses and a bikini that was two yellow belts of material stretched across her hips and nipples. She was tall and moved like a panther, and her body shone with oil. Her hair was purple at the roots but turned jet black and rose into a flat, razored rug. The top of her head resembled a golf tee. In one hand she held an ice-bucket and in the other a yapping terrier on a leash. The terrier was bouncing, and snapping at her ankles. 'Now cut that out, Orson,' she said, hooking the leash over a white, throne-shaped chair. She set down the ice-bucket, extracted a champagne bottle and ripped through the gold foil with long nails painted black.

She eased the cork. She said, 'Know what I hate?' She didn't wait
for a reply. 'I hate the fact that I wasn't here in the 1940s. My
friends are always saying to me: "Grace, you were born out of
time. You should have been here in the golden days." And you
know, I think they're right. Everyone took more care then.
Mayer, Selznick, and Cohn. Those guys had style. The stars had
style. The movies had style.' The cork was expelled with a bang. It
fizzed through the air, came down, bounced into the pool and
sank in the turgid, red water. Champagne foamed over her hands.
She said, 'That's what I hate. There's no such thing as Hollywood
now.'

'Dude,' said Norris. 'Check that wahini.'

The wahini gave us each a glass of champagne, and stared into
the pool. She said, 'Say, you two *are* the poolmen?'

'We're the poolmen,' confirmed Norris.

'It's gotten worse,' she said. This didn't seem to bother her. She
seemed fascinated by the water. 'It's really weird, you know, like
something from a horror movie.'

I said, 'What did you *do* to the pool, exactly?'

She shrugged. 'We woke up this morning and there it was.
Nicko says probably it's connected with the comet.'

'The comet?'

'You know, the one that appears every seventy years or so. All
sorts of weird stuff happens. Storms. Assassinations. Hit movies
at Columbia.'

'Halley's Comet.'

'That's it.'

But Halley's Comet, I said, had been and gone, last year.

'Yeah. But Nicko says it's gotta be around someplace, right?
Exerting an influence.'

'I see.'

'So what will you guys do? Can you fix it?'

Norris said, 'We can fix anything. We consider ourselves
artists. But this is a problem. It will require many treatments.'

I wondered why we couldn't just drain the pool, sluice it out,
and fill it up again.

'*Frequent* treatments,' said Norris.

'Just as long as the job gets done.'

'It'll get done,' said Norris, his eyes following the woman as she released the terrier, picked up the champagne bottle, and walked towards the house.

'Nice lady,' I said.

'A goddess, dude, a goddess.'

Now I understood why we couldn't just drain the pool. Norris would be planning at least five more visits. He invented these labyrinthine strategies to try and get to know women. Usually, the strategies failed, but he remained optimistic. He said that once, when he had been removing a dead chihuahua from a pool in Franklin Canyon, a complete stranger had invited him to an oral sex party which lasted three days.

'I've gotta get some scheme going on her,' said Norris.

I suggested that he could, perhaps, drown the dog.

Norris said I was lucky, having married a woman like Barbara. He asked how the marriage was turning out. 'Fine,' I said.

In fact it was a question that had been puzzling me as well. Barbara and I had been married for weeks and nothing had changed, not really. What happened in Las Vegas seemed surreal, like a dream. Barbara had taken off the ring two days after we got back. Tina, the Bunny Mother, had told her to do so. Bunnies might have been prohibited from dating customers, but it was also understood that they should not appear totally unavailable. Barbara now wore the ring round a chain on her neck. She said it was uncomfortable.

And there was something else. Things were going badly in bed. I kissed, I licked, I nibbled, I stroked, I sucked with eager lips, but before I could coax Barbara to orgasm, as soon as she locked her legs round my back, when, in short, she began to moan and grind, and bit my neck, when she began to show any sign of excitement, I yelled 'Geronimo' and was unable to prevent my own climax. It was driving me mad. Afterwards I would lie on top of Barbara, spent, ashamed. I didn't imagine she was feeling too pleased about it either. We avoided the subject.

'When I think of that dudely chick . . . ,' said Norris. 'Dude, you're totally out there, ripping it up, *shredding it*, dude.'

I said, 'Thanks.'

Barbara was delirious. She punched the air. She jigged up and down. She hugged her shoulders and made whooping noises like a police siren. She laughed and kissed me, saying: 'Let's do something. Let's take crystal methadrine. Let's call Moss. Let's go to Raging Waters.'

I said, 'What is Raging Waters?'

'I could party for days.'

'What happened?'

'Everything happened. I did a great audition, that's what happened. I did the Jane Fonda thing like you said, you were right about that, then they had me read with this guy, some scene from *Body Heat*, and then they gave me a camera test. Joel said I was the best they'd seen so far. Easily. They'll let me know in a few days. But Joel says I'm home free.'

I said, 'Who's Joel?'

'He's the director guy I told you about. Isn't it just the greatest? Are you gonna call Moss or shall I?'

I said I'd do it. Moss came round ten minutes later. Barbara told him the news and made more police-siren noises. I'd never seen her so excited. Moss offered his congratulations, Barbara grabbed a six-pack from the fridge, and we went outside to the car.

The Cadillac had been serviced: no more infested beer cans on the seats, no more *clunketa-clunketa* rumblings. The bodywork was polished and there were shining new hubcaps. Moss looked guilty, as though he'd betrayed a principle. He said, 'The machine was just gonna up and die if I didn't do something. It's not as if I went out and bought a BMW.'

We cruised south on Harbor Freeway. The top was down and the sky was dazzling, quivering in the heat. I thought the sky was about to melt. That could have been the effect of the crystal methadrine, which Barbara had given out as soon as we hit

Venice Boulevard and which made me feel weak, light-headed. I was in the back, in a drugged stupor. Barbara was in the front, in high spirits. She imitated the way the Cadillac used to sound, laughing and gesturing with a fanatic energy and enthusiasm. She talked about her happiness and ambition, telling Moss that now at last she'd fixed on something she wanted to do there would be no stopping her. She tried to describe how she felt in front of the camera. She said it was better than sex.

Raging Waters was in Anaheim. The plastic snow which capped the Matterhorn in Disneyland could be seen from the parking lot. Raging Waters cost $15 and was another kind of amusement park. 'Hours of Aquatic Fun' and 'Honk if You're a Swimmer' said the posters. There were chutes and slides, swings and helter-skelters, spiralling ramps and twisting tunnels, all filled with thunderous water and yelling, shooting bodies. It seemed dangerous. I viewed a steepling helter-skelter called Foam Frolic and knew my stomach wasn't up to this. Moss voiced similar reservations. 'Wimps,' said Barbara.

Moss and I took off our shoes and socks. We dangled our feet in Toddlers' Pool and swigged from a bottle of bourbon we had hidden in a brown Ralph's bag. In front of us a thick-bodied man, small and swarthy, pulled on giant black flippers, strapped paddles to his wrists, plugged a waterproof Sony in his ears, pulled goggles over his eyes and a silver bathing cap over his greying hair. Moss and I agreed he was taking things too far. Moss asked if he was trying for a part in *20,000 Leagues Under the Sea*. The man slapped his feet towards a bubbling maelstrom called Whippy's Whirlpool. He turned and sneered: 'You two looking for the *little boys'* room?' He leaped into the maelstrom, and vanished.

Barbara came back from the changing room. She wore a white swimsuit made of faintly luminous material, pushed her lustrous hair into a Speedo cap and when a curl sprang loose tucked it back in with a deft motion of thumb and forefinger.

'Watch me,' she said.

'A pleasure,' said Moss.

She climbed the aluminium ladder which ran up the side of the Foam Frolic helter-skelter. Standing on the platform at the top, she waved, and threw herself head first down the chute. Moments later she was at the bottom, entering the water like an arrow, a blur of white and tanned flesh.

Moss said, 'What do you think success does? Does it change people straight off, or does it sneak up slow and gradual, and before you know it's been happening, bang, you're a different person?'

I told him I'd once met the actor Mickey Rourke, in a boxing club in Whitechapel, in the East End of London. The place smelled of liniment and sweat. I was researching a feature and Rourke was there, unshaven, wearing boxing gloves, lounging across the ropes of the ring. He'd been working out and he was breathing heavily. This was a couple of years before he became famous but there was something about the way he stood and looked: he was already a star, he knew it was going to happen. He was confident, at ease. He knew what he would become, and was preparing for the role.

'You felt the same thing with Barbara?'

'In a way.'

Moss asked how I'd feel if Barbara became a success. I thought about it. I wasn't sure. I'd never imagined her in *someone else's* movie.

We took more crystal methadrine. We drove to Brentwood, to The No-Name Bar on San Vicente, a place which had only been open a few weeks and was built in imitation of the *Cheers* TV show: three-sided bar, wood tables and dark oak chairs, bare boards on the floor and sports pennants on the walls. Everything smelled new. Barbara went to make a phone call.

'Tastes like a tyre,' a man at the bar was saying, pushing away a plate that carried a barely touched hamburger. 'Tell Bernice she didn't grill this burger. She leased it from Goodyear.' The man had a broad lined face and a forehead to beat down doors with. He turned to Moss and me. He told us his name was Horace

Schwartz and that Bernice was the chef here. A month ago he had predicted the sex of her child. He had said it would be human. Schwartz bought us drinks, and when he discovered I was English asked if I found Los Angeles amusing.

'That's not quite the word,' I said.

Schwartz said, 'LA's all right so long as you remember that when Chandler said it was a city with the personality of a paper cup he intended a compliment. I read a story once that said, "She came to LA and the whole of her life turned to chaos." Actually, I wrote the story.'

'You're a writer?'

He nodded. He said he'd written a film for the Beatles, one for Cary Grant, another for Robert Mitchum, a modern-day vampire story, a surreal comedy about the rise and fall of Nazism, and a novel in the form of a murderous travelogue across America, featuring a death in every state. Now he took other people's scripts and turned the sentences around: 'I demand the right to a lawyer;' 'Bring me a lawyer'; 'I want a lawyer and I want him quick'. He made out. He and his wife had a bungalow up on Carmelina, postage-stamp lawn out front and patio out back. His children were grown up. One was a dentist, the other was in accounting at Disney. Neither believed that he had once met Cary Grant. They thought he was eccentric.

Barbara was back, demanding alcohol. She swiped a glass from the bar and downed it in one. I introduced her to Schwartz. I said, 'He wrote a Beatles movie.'

'The words will be on my tombstone,' he said.

Barbara said, 'Who did you like best, John or Paul?'

'Didn't meet either. I dealt with the director.'

Barbara was impressed. She said, 'My father got tickets for Shea Stadium. He took my mom. They were at college then. He was telling me about it a couple of months back. He says he remembers the smell of girls wetting their pants.'

'Your dad a music fan?' said Moss.

'He used to be. Still is. He's dead now.'

'He still is?'

Barbara smiled. 'You got it.'

Moss looked bemused.

A TV above the bar was on, showing basketball, a game in the NBA play-offs. A Laker, I think it was Byron Scott, dispossessed an opponent and moved down the court to score. Schwartz was telling Barbara about the film he'd written for Cary Grant, a comedy adventure set in the capitals of Europe. It was one of those stories where the audience was supposed to be in the dark about whether Cary Grant was the good guy or the bad guy, except any audience would know he was the good guy simply because he was Cary Grant, even if he did wear suits that glowed in the dark. He made it sound very complicated. He told her he had lived in Europe for many years and described the house he once had with his family outside Brussels, a rambling cottage with two windows that were like huge eyes when they reflected the sky above the flat, brown landscape. His face assumed a rueful expression. He said, 'For about a year I was very big in Belgium.'

I half-listened. My head throbbed from the drugs and booze and sun. I needed sleep, badly. I glanced towards the door and thought I was hallucinating. I clutched Barbara's shoulder.

I said, 'I thought I just saw Patterson walk in.'

'Who's Patterson?' said Schwartz.

'An old friend,' said Barbara.

'It's not him, is it?' I said.

'He's late.'

'Late?'

'Said he'd be here ten minutes ago.'

'What?'

She gave me a kooky grin. 'It's a big night for me. I wanted him to come celebrate. He's a good buddy.'

A good buddy?

Patterson came up. He had trimmed his beard and wore a black leather jacket which smelled as though it had once belonged to a motor-cycle gang member unconcerned with personal hygiene. Barbara made the introductions.

'And here's Richard,' she said. 'Richard, you know.'

'Yeah,' said Patterson, 'Richard, I know,' and he gave me an unpleasant smile. He turned to Horace Schwartz. 'I think I've heard your name. Don't you have credits?'

Schwartz beamed wih pleasure at the recognition. Barbara smiled, as if to say: *Isn't this marvellous?*

I tried to regain my composure. Moss was asking Schwartz about writing music for films. Was it tough to break into? Did he have any contacts? How much did composers get paid for writing scores? Patterson moved in beside me at the bar. He said he wanted to make a bet. I could decide the stake – $1,000, $5,000, even $20,000, anything I liked. That was up to me.

'What's the bet?'

'You know,' said Patterson.

'I do?'

'That I'll win in the end.'

'Win *what?*'

Patterson said he'd never give up. I said I didn't know what he was talking about.

'You just decide on the bet, Richard,' he said. 'And I'll take the money. There are things about Barbara you'll never know.'

Barbara said, 'You two getting friendly at last?'

'That's it,' said Patterson. 'Me and Richard are gonna be real good buddies.' He punched me on the arm, playfully. He told me a joke about a screenwriter he knew who had never been to bed with a woman in his life. Patterson became the life and soul of the party.

Barbara suggested we go to the Lhasa Club in West Hollywood. She said, 'Let's take more crystal methadrine. Lots more. Lots and lots.'

I groaned. I felt dreadful. I felt (I know I've said this before) confused. What *was* crystal methadrine?

That night I dreamed I was lost, walking through an empty movie lot. There were shops with names like Nick's Groceries, the Laredo Saloon and Will's Livery Stable. The sun was blistering.

At the end of a street I found a car, a red sports car, and a woman in a bikini was stretched on the bonnet. She made a gun with her thumb and forefinger, saying 'Bang. You're shot.' It was Barbara, who told me I had to go to Lot 55. She did not tell me where Lot 55 was. I carried on. I was filthy with dust and sweat. I came to a wall of red clay with a small, circular entrance like a burrow. There was a sign: 'Lot 55 – strictly no unauthorized personnel'. I went in. I was in a tunnel, dark, hot and narrow. It pulsed like a human throat. Ropes hung from the ceiling and stuck to my flesh as I pushed through. From the end of the tunnel came an echoing voice: 'Pirates and bikini women prepare to jump.' Beyond the tunnel was a space as huge as the inside of a cathedral. There were cranes, cameras on wheels, and floodlights. Generators whirred and grey smoke billowed over a lake. Squads of men thwacked the lake with paddles, sending oily water lapping over the partly submerged hull of a ship. Figures in pirate suits and bikinis perched on a ledge, waiting to jump. The director was young, with a beard and protruding eyes: Patterson. He brandished a white megaphone. 'Bikini women, ready,' he shouted, 'bikini women . . . *jump*,' and they did, and each one was Barbara. I took Patterson by the shoulders. Didn't he understand? I was the penis man. He told me not to be so bloody ridiculous. I screamed, 'I *am* the penis man.'

I woke in a chair, back at our apartment. I was still dressed. My back ached, my throat rasped and my tongue was swollen. My mouth seemed to be lined with fungus. My head wore the iron hat and my memory was a jingle-jangle of events in the latter stages of the previous evening. It had turned into a stampede. I remembered a dizzying drive to Hollywood, an entry into a dank, subterranean nightclub, a band that sounded like hell, the consumption of more alcohol, more drugs. I seemed also to recall (could this really have happened?) lying on top of a bar beneath a whisky bottle, pressing a greedy mouth against the optic, and trying to tell someone about a story I wanted to write, about an artist who lived with his mother in Finsbury Park and had to be fed raw liver and fairy stories twice a day. After that: a blank.

It was midday. I was alone in the apartment. This was

worrying. I had the feeling I had behaved very badly. Perhaps Barbara had been angry, and not come home. Perhaps she was with Patterson.

I splashed water in my face. I looked in the cupboards for coffee. There was none. I decided to go out for breakfast. On Venice Boulevard a truck thundered by. Palm trees with hairstyles like Rod Stewart rattled in the wind. A police car – doors open, lights flashing – was outside the El As de Oros and two uniformed police had someone up against a wall with his legs spread at twenty past eight. The sun scorched my eyes and my brains seemed about to froth out of my head like sherbet: they were restrained only by the iron hat which was clamped round my skull and now tightening. I fumbled for my sunglasses.

I walked to Culver City. Ship's Diner was an old (i.e. 1957) place with a neon sign in the shape of a rocket. The waitresses were ageing Kim Novaks. On each table was a toaster from the age when fins were put on everything. I sat in a booth in the corner, ordered coffee, orange juice and toast, and looked over the LA Times. On page 27 I read:

ENGLISH TOURIST KILLED BY BAT

English holidaymaker Thomas Walker has died in Beverly Glen Hospital, eight days after being attacked by a rabid bat, medical authorities revealed yesterday. Walker was driving in Benedict Canyon with Elizabeth Walker, his wife, when the incident occurred. Mrs Walker said, 'I don't know where the bats came from. We had the top down and they swooped suddenly. They bit my husband repeatedly about the face and neck. It was his first visit to California. He'd been looking forward to it so much. It was his dream. Now he'll be buried here.' The incidence of bat attack in the Beverly Hills area has increased fifty per cent over last year's figure. Mr Walker will be cremated tomorrow, 3 p.m., in the Hollywood Cemetery.

Bat attacks and bunny girls: Los Angeles, it seemed, was giving it to the English in a big way. I pushed toast into my mouth and sucked up coffee, wondering whether I should go to Thomas

Walker's funeral, express sympathy, tell the widow that I knew how she felt, that California wasn't making life a bed of roses for me either. After all, we English should stick together.

On the booth to my left a woman described the new Woody Allen movie. She was saying, 'I guess you'd say it's like this really humorous collection of vignettes. First of all there's a vignette, I can't really remember what it's about, but it's humorous, really very humorous indeed, and then something else happens, a scene, or a vignette I guess you'd call it, and that's pretty funny as well, and then another vignette that had me laughing a lot. It's just a series of vignettes, I suppose, but very humorous. I think Woody's neat, so neat, don't you?'

Another voice said: 'May I sit here?'

I looked up. The speaker was a short, slim man with greying hair and a blue suit. He was black, and he had a metal claw where his right hand should have been. I said, 'That'll be fine,' and he sat opposite, reaching out with the claw to grab a menu. He saw my stare.

'Excuse me.'

He smiled, saying he was used to it. His name was Bennett Ramsay and he was a Culver City attorney. He lost the hand in Vietnam. Nothing dramatic, he said, not a combat wound, he was supervising the unloading of a transport plane and a crate slipped, smashing his arm. He never even knew what was in the crate. He was sent home to Philadelphia. He found that city 'too weird' (he didn't elaborate) so he got on a Greyhound bus, headed west, and took the California bar exams. After he qualified he spent ten years with a firm of entertainment lawyers in Hollywood and then set up his own practice.

Ike Turner had been one of his clients. He said, 'I represented him in the divorce from Tina. Was one of the worst jobs I ever had. Ike was a mean guy and I mean *really* mean. He was wild, crazy, evil. He talked dirty, he talked filthy, he talked crap. He used to rave about how he'd found Tina when she was a fourteen-year-old whore in South St Louis and how he'd made her what she is today, about how she owed him everything. He'd say, "I *own* Tina." I told him there was something in this country called the thirteenth amendment which prohibited slavery. He didn't take too kindly to that and I tell you I was worried 'cos I knew all the time he was just crazy enough to arrange for some of his friends to come round and hurt me. He used to show at the court in a grey Cadillac, wearing a grey Homburg hat and a grey silk suit. Guy looked like a pimp. Tina was as cool and demure as any woman I ever saw. When she wasn't in court she'd curl up on a bench outside and sleep like a baby. One night I got a call from Tina's lawyer. She asked why I couldn't keep my client under control. Ike had just been round to Tina's house, blown out the windows of her car with a shotgun.'

I thought about the story. I wondered how many men there were who, in some wild moment, hadn't imagined doing something like that, a script that went along the following lines: 'You're not going to do what I want? No? Well eat *this*, bitch.' I thought about the movies I'd been shooting in my head for years, movies of passion, movies of obsession, movies in which some real woman would take a role, only for me to find that she'd start usurping the character I'd created for her.

Bennett Ramsay was saying, 'Yeah, that Ike, he was some kind of a guy. He used to say, "I own Tina, man. She's my *drugstore*." '

Barbara came back at four-thirty. She juggled red carrier bags, with 'I Love To Shop' on the side. I inspected her face for signs of a hangover. Unbelievably, there were none. She seemed in a bad mood. She said she had risen early, got back her car from the garage, and gone to Santa Monica. She rummaged in a bag and tossed me a parcel. I ripped through crinkling paper and found a black shirt, decorated with huge, green flowers.

'Thanks,' I said.

'You're welcome,' she said in a cool voice.

I considered launching a pre-emptive strike, making a blanket apology for whatever I might have done the previous night, but decided to wait. I didn't have to wait long.

She said, 'Boy, you were out of it.'

'Oh,' I said.

Barbara proceeded to catalogue my misdemeanours. I had made myself conspicuous by throwing martini olives at other customers in the Lhasa Club. I had indeed been found lying on top of the bar, trying to drink from a bottle (tequila, not whisky). I had become boring, talking in a loud voice of the books I wished to write. It seemed I had also given Barbara a hard time about the fact that she'd invited Patterson to the No-Name Bar, calling her, among other names, a bag, a bitch, a bimbo. I had challenged Patterson to a duel.

She said, 'Patterson nearly died laughing.'

I thought, I bet he did.

'Then you crashed. Out cold. We had to carry you to the car,' she said. She kissed me. 'You've got to lighten up, Richard.'

It had been even worse than I feared. *A duel?* I wondered what sort of wild Sidney Carton fantasy had been going through my mind at that point.

Breakfast with the McCreas: it happened once a fortnight and 'Angels of the Poolside' employees were invited in rotation. Attendance was expected and it was the turn of Norris and Rayner. The essential thing, Norris warned, was to say as little as possible, hope for a quick getaway.

'Is it that bad?'

'Wait and see, dude.'

The McCrea residence was a pink bungalow on Rose Avenue in Palms. Plaster statues of Jesus and the Virgin Mary were on the lawn and a message pinned to the door said: 'Prayer–Penance–Atonement, The Choice Is Yours!' Norris rang the bell, which chimed the Agnus Dei from Mozart's Coronation Mass. Norris said, 'Cute.'

McCrea opened the door. There was a dab of reddened tissue paper on his jutting chin. Perhaps he'd cut himself shaving. An apron was stretched tight across his barrel chest and he held a meat cleaver. His appearance was gruesome.

'Just preparing the meal,' he said, grinning, beckoning us into the room behind him. He made it sound as though he was getting ready for the Apocalypse. We went in. There was a breakfast bar, a long sofa in pink leather and the smell of meat cooking. Lights that resembled organ pipes hung from the ceiling. The thick pile carpet was imperial purple. So was the wallpaper, though in one corner this was stained a darker colour by damp. The stain was in the shape of South America, and above it was a framed photograph of a nuclear mushroom.

'I want you to meet my wife,' said McCrea, still brandishing the meat cleaver. 'The Virgin speaks to the world through Marlene. Through her we walk with God.'

As if on cue a woman came into the room. She was small and pretty and wore a yellow silk dress. Her feet were bare. She had brown eyes set wide apart and dark hair which curled away at the shoulders. Her skin was very pale. I had never met a religious fanatic. Was this what they looked like?

'James,' she said to Norris, taking his elbows and kissing him on the cheek. Her voice was surprisingly deep. 'And you must be Richard.' She held my hands and examined me, starting at my feet and working slowly up my body, as if looking for the cracks. This went on for a long time. I wasn't sure if I could keep a straight face, and Norris gave me a warning glare.

McCrea said, 'Marlene likes to do this with strangers. She's tuning in, she's getting your number.'

Marlene smiled and thanked me. I felt like I was sliding on ice.

McCrea said, 'Who's hungry?'

'I could eat,' said Norris.

'And so could I,' I said.

We sat on stools at the breakfast bar. McCrea closed his eyes, dipped his head, and Marlene said grace: 'The chastisement will be great but man must understand. There must be another chastisement. And this great chastisement will come from man, through the hands of a man, and it will be a war so great it will exterminate the earth, but for the merciful heart of the Eternal Father and the chastisement of the ball of redemption.'

She kept repeating that word, *chastisement*, with relish. What was she going on about? I stared at Norris, raising my eyebrows.

He stared back, expressionless. She continued, 'Bless this food O merciful Father and purge us all for the time of chastisement. Amen.'

'Amen,' boomed McCrea.

'Amen,' said Norris.

'Amen,' I echoed.

McCrea laid out plates on the breakfast bar's pink formica top. The plates were loaded with fruit, cheese, bread and varieties of ham and salami. Another held a steaming pile of salt beef.

I said, 'What is the chastisement of the ball of redemption?'

The question went down big. Norris frowned. McCrea smiled like an idiot. Marlene put butter on a crispbread, spreading it with quick flicks of the wrist. Her hands were slender and delicate. She said, 'The great conflagration. Armageddon'

I said I didn't understand.

She pointed her knife at the photograph in the corner of the room. She said, 'Nuclear war.'

'Nuclear war?'

She nodded.

'But that's terrible.'

'Oh yes, Richard, it is terrible,' she said. 'But it has to come. It will come. The Word has been spoken. It has been through me.'

I wondered why she had to seem so cheerful about it.

McCrea explained the game plan. The Virgin Mary had spoken to Marlene, told her the world would soon be cleansed by nuclear war. Evil would be swept away and the survivors would start afresh according to God's will. All would be darkness and fiery confusion. He said he was disappointed that so many people in Los Angeles were ignorant and uncaring of this message. He had come up with the solution: a television network. He was raising the money now. In a year or so he would wrap up the business, sell the house, and move into a motor-home. He said, 'The Lord spoke to me just the one time. He said one word. "Television".'

Television. McCrea and his wife were a riot. I tried to change the subject. I said to Norris, 'What do you think? Can the Lakers go all the way?'

Marlene said I needn't be embarrassed. I shouldn't be afraid of her message. I should confront the reality of the situation. It would make me a happier individual. She took my hand and gazed into my palm. She said, 'Richard, I sense you are a very troubled young man.'

McCrea guffawed. She'd got my number all right.

Afterwards, in the van, Norris said: 'Dude, we're talking big-league craziness here. McCrea was born in 1947, born again in 1981, and again in 1982, and again every six months after that.'

We were heading for Mulholland Drive, back to the house with the swimming pool which resembled a bath full of blood. Norris was continuing his pursuit of the panther woman. I told him he was being unrealistic, but Norris said, 'Buff woman. Surfer chick.'

We stopped at a red light on National. A black Chrysler pulled up alongside. The driver wore a pork-pie hat and worked a toothpick between his teeth. A sticker on the back window said: 'Honk if you're Jesus.'

Barbara wanted to go to the beach. Her expression told me it would be unwise to object. We drove to Malibu. Part of Coast Highway was fenced off, and the road was strewn with boulders which had fallen from the cliffs. Barbara told me several people were killed here each year, crushed.

We stopped at a shop called Zuma Jay's. Barbara wanted sunglasses. Inside there was the sickly smell of surfboard wax. The man behind the counter looked like the actor Oscar Homolka. He had bushy eyebrows and jowly cheeks. He was in his forties, and a rug of greying chest hair sprouted over the neck of his T-shirt. He had a cigar clamped between his teeth and a theory. The theory concerned why smoking was about to be banned in Beverly Hills. He said, 'At the end of World War Two those Nazis went to South America. Now they control the tobacco industry, right? And the movie industry is run by Jews. Who all live in Beverly Hills. You see what I'm saying? They're getting their revenge. That's what it's all about. You used the ovens, we don't buy the smokes. Simple.'

Barbara had chosen a pair of wrap-around Ray-Bans. 'You look *hot*. Just like Clint in *Dirty Harry*,' said the man behind the counter. 'When I die I'm gonna be cremated on my surfboard. Wearing my shades. Can you dig it? Like a Viking. This buddy of mine, he was swallowed by a shark, *whole*. They caught the fish about a week later and my buddy was still inside, rotting. They couldn't even take his wet suit off, it was just sort of *moulded* to his skin. Can you imagine that happening to your body? That's just totally gross. I'm taking the burning option. It's Valhalla for me.'

Barbara gave him a cool stare as she handed over a credit card. She said, 'Butt out, pal.'

He said, 'OK, lady, no offence, just shooting off at the mouth as usual. Me, I like the Jews *and* the Nazis.'

We bought doughnuts and a quart of milk from a 7-Eleven, and walked to the beach. Barbara was silent. Graffiti on a wall said 'Nathan Pratt is back' and 'Fight sewers'. Who was Nathan Pratt? Barbara shrugged. I didn't need to ask about the sewers. A few hundred yards north, the Malibu Colony was a paradise of $2m homes and security systems, but the beach was filthy. At its edge was a mountainous heap of seaweed and debris, exhaling a rotting smell. Barbara and I sat upwind, watching the surfers come in off the point. Far out to sea there was a huge oil tanker, motionless.

Barbara sat on a towel, knees hugged to her face, tight as a spring.

I said, 'What's the matter?'

She said, 'Can't you guess?'

Cancer . . .? Patterson . . .? AIDS . . .? Bankruptcy . . .? Massive social stigma attendant on being often in the company of a non-driving Englishman . . .? Sex . . .? I said, 'No.'

She dug her fingers in the sand. 'I didn't get the part in the movie.'

She hadn't got the part: I felt relieved, then ashamed about being relieved. I told her there would be other parts, as I watched an old man, he must have been seventy, walk towards the ocean, surfboard tucked under one arm, eating an ice-cream. 'Don't let it get to you.'

Barbara's fingers plunged deeper into the sand. Behind the sunglasses her face seemed resolute. She said, 'I won't. I'm gonna show them.' She spoke in a monotone. She said she was going to Orange County at the weekend. She wanted to forget the whole business. Her sister would be there. She was staying for a few days in a beach house at San Juan Capastrano. It had been a long time since they'd seen each other. They would have plenty to talk about. I could come if I wanted, but I'd have to keep out of the way.

I knew the sisters were very friendly. Kimberley had been with Barbara in Crete. I didn't meet her. She was up in the mountains when I was there. Barbara told me they had been companions in various escapades. They had travelled together by train across Canada, and had acted in an amateur production of *West Side Story*. Once they had stolen a big Trans-Am sports car and gone joyriding. They had been stopped by the highway patrol. The cops had been amazed, and had surprisingly told Barbara and Kimberley they would let them go, just so long as they used this hot car to go harass some faggots.

I had no such shared experience with my brother and sister. Both were several years older. People told me I was like my brother. He had been expelled from school (the usual things – disobedience, non-attendance, drugs), spent five years as the drummer in an unsuccessful rock band which seemed always to be *about* to make it, managed a clothes shop, then switched career and became a lawyer. He had been a teenage delinquent, he once said, I caught the habit later on. Both of us dreaded that we might end up like our father (i.e. in trouble, in debt, *in jail*) yet cherished the fantasy of the outlaw life, both of us wore spectacles and liked *Citizen Kane*, Charles Dickens, Len Deighton and early Phil Spector records, and we were both married, though Todd didn't know about Barbara and me. No one in England knew about that. I thought about Jane. What would she say if she found out? She probably wouldn't believe it. She'd been wanting us to get married for nearly two years. I'd told her marriage was a boring institution.

Barbara said, 'Maybe Kimberley and me'll get Patterson's gun, go *shoot* this director guy. That'd sure teach him for not putting me in his movie.' She dived into her bag, came up with a bottle of varnish, unscrewed the top and began to paint her nails. The shade was called 'Scarlett's Revenge'.

The trip began with a detour. We looped through Pacific Palisades and headed north, stopping for petrol at a 76 station near Malibu. A rusty Ford Valiant came up behind us on the forecourt and six teenagers poured out, armed with hacksaws, and tore the roof off the car. Then they took spray-guns and applied paint in bursts of red and yellow. The car came in as an old sedan, left as a convertible with a psychedelic paint-job, and the entire process was over before I'd filled the Mustang's tank.

I wanted to go to Zuma Beach, to inspect the crumbling arch through which the surfers make their entrance at the end of the John Milius film *Big Wednesday*, this was one of my favourite movies. When we were there, I told Barbara: 'It's about the loss of innocence. At the beginning the heroes are surf bums. One gets sent to Vietnam. They don't see each other for years. They endure pain and loss. A friend is killed. At the end they all meet here because they know an enormous wave is coming in. They ride it. It's their moment of greatness. It redeems everything else in their lives. Wouldn't it be terrific to have something like that?'

Barbara said I should hear myself sometimes.

We turned round and went south on Coast Highway, past Malibu and the Bel-Air Beach Club where a red-waistcoated valet parked a Porsche with the registration 'IM WIRED', through Santa Monica and Venice Beach, skirting LAX where tubby airliners jockeyed for take-off and the air was heavy with the smell of jet fuel, past an enormous oil refinery with the sun glinting off storage tanks and row after row of nodding donkeys, until finally we bumped and swooped down a hill into Manhattan Beach. We stopped for lunch.

In the Mr Fat Boy Diner a man with sunglasses and strange blue marks on the backs of his hands told us he was thinking of emigrating to Russia. He said he was serious. 'Buddy, you can earn $1,500 roubles a month, guaranteed. Or China. I hear things are pretty good there too. What's that you say? What's the dollar equivalent of 1,500 roubles? How should I know? You think I'm the *Wall St Journal*? So I said to the foreman, "I'm thinking of quitting. I'm thinking of going to Russia." He said he'd buy me a dictionary. He said he'd find out about plane times for me. Can you believe that? I'm gonna tear that guy five new assholes. Say, lady, would you care to suck my penis?'

Barbara didn't even pause to appraise the size. We moved to a table by the window, and ordered coffee and ice-cream. Barbara told me a story about her father. She remembered sitting on his knee while he peeled an orange with a clasp-knife and the skin came off in one piece, coiled like a snake. She said, 'Everything he did, he did it real well. I guess I should try and live that way. Like acting. If I want to do it I should really go for it, don't you think?'

'Can I ask you something?'

'Shoot.'

'I've wanted to ask you for a long time. When you say your father comes and talks to you, it's in your dreams, in your imagination, right?'

'Wrong,' she said. 'It's real.'

'That's impossible.'

'It's very possible.'

'It can't be real.'

'It's as real as talking to you now.'

On the other side of the street an old woman stopped outside a bookstore. She wore mauve ankle socks and looked frail. She punched the window, once and then again. She kept doing it: *jab-jab-jab*. The glass began to wobble and bounce, reflecting streaks of sky. She went on, *jab-jab-jab, jab-jab, jab-jab-jab* until the window disintegrated and sparkling glass showered over her.

'As real as you and me fucking.' Barbara thrust a spoon deep into her chocolate sundae.

We drove on. After Hermosa and Redondo Beach our route wiggled inland, slicing off the Palos Verdes peninsula, then it was back to the coast. In Long Beach we inspected the *Queen Mary* and the world's biggest seaplane, built by Howard Hughes, a jumbo-sized mistake with about thirty engines which had flown only once and was now moored in a warehouse. We saw a group of men outside a BMW showroom. They wore suits and ties, and hats with feathers in the band. They looked like salesmen and practised golf shots: balls fizzed into the ocean. Barbara spotted a Rolls-Royce with smoked windows and a tiger-skin design on the roof, which she said must belong to a pimp. She said, 'There's a black gang here. They drive around in cars like that.'

I looked at Barbara. Her eyes were fixed on the road. How did she know all this stuff? She was always surprising me. I remembered Patterson's boast that there were things about her I'd never know. Perhaps he was right. Barbara and I were, I had to admit, having our problems, such as failure to understand each other, lack of common experience, and bad sex. On the other hand we *were* married, and possession was nine-tenths of the law. Let Patterson put that in his pipe and smoke it.

It was hot and sunny as we crossed into Orange County. To the east of Coast Highway there was a flat, desolate swamp. A sign said this was Seal Beach Naval Weapons Research Unit. Barbara said this was where the CIA trained dolphins to kill Russians: 'They put these little bombs in their noses.'

I remembered the story Norris had told me. I said, 'Someone in Beverly Hills has one of these dolphins in their swimming pool.'

Barbara told me not to be ridiculous.

We picked up a hitch-hiker. He looked at Barbara and thought it was his lucky day. He saw me and his face dropped. He tossed a rucksack onto the back seat, climbed in beside it, and Barbara roared off. He had freckles and seemed very young. He wore paisley-patterned beach shorts and a green shirt with an alligator on the chest. He was a media studies major at UC Irvine and his name was Jerry Sturgeon, which brought a laugh from Barbara.

He had an eerie self-assurance. His life was mapped out. He talked of college, career, marriage and 'potential later partici- pation in the arena of politics'.

He said, 'I've got this beautiful plan. Imagine: roll back history 10 million years. It'll be the biggest TV event of all time, the biggest ever. I'm gonna send a space probe to this secret canyon on Mars. The probe will be loaded with TV equipment, lasers, all that good shit, state of the art technology, and the trip will be beamed back to earth. Live. Everyone pays $50 for the cable link up. $50 for the adventure of the century! Cheap at the price. I'm calling it "The Martian Experience". Cost $300m, $400m tops.'

'Where will you get the money?' I asked. He said that would be no problem. He was rich. He was worth $45m on the hoof. 'And what's in the canyon?' I said.

'Nobody knows,' he said. 'That's the adventure. Maybe just a bunch of rocks. Maybe not. Maybe there's a lost world out there, dinosaurs slugging it out toe-to-toe, like one of those movies.'

Barbara wasn't buying any of this. She asked why, if he was so rich, on or off the hoof, he happened to be begging a ride on Coast Highway.

'Experience,' he said. 'I have three cars. I don't have to do this. I do this for the experience. I've been all the way across country, four times. Like those guys in that book. Except I put my experience to good use. I make notes on everything.'

He unzipped the rucksack and took out three spiral-bound notebooks. They were blue, and he waved them under my nose. He said these were his bibles. Number one he called 'Personal Relationships', number two was 'Business – Advice, Information, Conquest', while number three featured 'General Tips'. He gave an example. Once he broke down on an interstate in Montana. He was miles from the nearest town. A truck came by. The driver was a mechanic, with a PhD from a university in Germany somewhere. He called himself 'The Diesel Doctor'. It turned out that he was the only man within two hundred miles who could have fixed the car. That went in book number two.

He said, 'I'll be up in Montana on business someday. I may need that guy. He told me there was no speed limit on the freeways in Germany, and if you take your wallet with you to a hooker in Hamburg, you could get killed for it. "General Tips". Stuff like this, it could save your life.' He patted the notebook.

He said, 'What about you guys? What's the deal here? You dating or what?'

I stared at him. He pushed a stick of Juicy Fruit into his mouth. 'We're married,' I said.

'You don't *look* married,' he said, chewing on the gum.

Barbara held up the chain with the ring.

'Dead cats,' said Jerry Sturgeon, and I wondered what sort of conversational gambit that might be. He continued: 'I met this guy in Philadelphia. He was driving a sky-blue Cadillac. Every time someone brought him a dead cat he'd give them a ring just like that. Said they cost him a buck apiece. He used the fur to make bathroom rugs.'

'You don't say,' said Barbara, and suggested he keep quiet.

He ignored this. He asked more questions. He wanted to know all about Barbara and me. Where had we met? What had we talked about? Where had we married? Had it been a long engagement? Had we drawn up a contract in the event of divorce? What was the wedding chapel like? Were our parents alive? When had we first fucked?

He went on and on. I asked myself what it would take to shut him up. My mind turned to threats, violence, assassination.

He said, 'And now that you're married, I guess the screwing is lousy, like everybody says.'

The Mustang veered off the road. It slid to a halt in front of a derelict cinema. Torn posters advertised surf movies. My face stopped inches short of the windscreen, then the safety belt garotted me back into my seat. Barbara assured Jerry Sturgeon he would regret it for the rest of his days unless he left *right now*.

'Excuse me?' he said.

'Get the fuck out of the car,' said Barbara. 'Otherwise I'll chop your balls off.'

And suddenly Jerry Sturgeon was outside the cinema, wearing an aggrieved expression, and the Mustang was accelerating away.

'No more hitch-hikers,' said Barbara.

'Dead right,' I said, wondering whether we feature in the first, second or third of Jerry Sturgeon's bibles.

We drove on, ducking down a hill into Laguna Beach, past Chuck's Chicklet Diner, Yoda's Nursery, the Aztec Motor Lodge and a concrete basketball-court where a tall, extremely thin white played one-on-one with a tall, equally emaciated black who slammed the ball into the basket, shouting 'In your face'. We parked and walked on the beach. It was late afternoon: sun dipping into the purply-blue ocean, shadows deepening on the sun-coloured mountains behind, beachgoers assembling their gear and preparing to leave. I noticed the same old man we'd seen at Malibu a few days before. He had a tanned, weathered face and a long, pointy nose. He wore a bathing cap with '33' on the side. Barbara asked what the number meant and he said that was the year he first surfed this beach, 1933. He had lots of caps, one for each of the different beaches up and down the coast: Rincon, Tressles, Huntington, Old Man's, San Onofre, Sunset, Seal.

He said, 'I was up at Rincon one time, this would have been about 1940, and there was a car coming down the hill. So I got out in the road with a blanket and started playing matador. The car swerved and went fishtailing down the highway, right over the sea wall. The driver wasn't hurt. It was some kind of a miracle. Another time I surfed on the pedestal of the fountain outside Hermosa High School. I was naked at the time. Traffic going by, bimbos staring. I used to be quite a wild young man.

'I think of the old days, standing up on the board and seeing the bottom go by, octopus and abalone down below. Now you get shit in the sea, and oil, and trash. This used to be a beautiful country.'

That night we stayed at the San Clemente Travel Inn. Afterwards, Barbara said, 'Maybe if you didn't try so hard, maybe if you relaxed . . .' I sat on the edge of the bed, gazing at the wall where there were marks like squashed fruit: dead mosquitoes, perhaps? I felt numb.

The next morning we bumped along a dirt road that ran between a railway track and the beach. The place where Kimberley was staying was a red two-storeyed house, built from wood. We went in. There was an open-plan living area, blue carpet on the floor, and an atmosphere of hysteria: people dancing, people rushing out of sliding doors onto a deck which overlooked the ocean, people milling around a table where a device of gleaming steel fountained tequila into salt-rimmed glasses. A middle-aged man with a gaunt face like James Stewart's stood in the centre of the room, rocking to and fro, practising his tennis serve, and a man in baggy white shorts described how he'd seen someone win the jackpot on a slot machine in Atlantic City. He performed it, jerking the lever, waiting, stepping back with open mouth, hands punching the air as invisible coins gushed out.

Someone was saying: 'We had to do Grenada, wasn't much involved but we had to do it . . .'

Another voice: 'He was there on business, the kiss and make up . . .'

'Now what the British did against Argentina in the Falklands. That was an operation . . .'

'. . . of course, he's as rich as God.'

'Argentina. Is that where the ponchos are?'

'If we went into Afghanistan, then you'd be talking?'

'Where *is* Afghanistan?'

Barbara shouldered through the crowd. She yelled, 'Kimberley, Kimber-LEEEE.'

'Think I'll come live down here. I'm sick of LA,' someone announced. 'It's chaos there, man. Total . . . chaos.'

The gaunt man like James Stewart came up. His manner was shy and diffident. He was extremely tall. 'Yeah . . . ah . . . OK . . .' he stuttered. 'Bloody Mary?'

'No thanks,' I said. I'd never been able to drink the stuff. It was a pity: an *alcoholic* drink to make you feel better while suffering from dreadful hangovers had an obvious appeal. I said, 'It's the texture of the tomato juice. Like human flesh passed through a Magimix. It makes me want to throw up.'

He seemed appalled by this. He frowned, lobbed an imaginary ball, smacked it over a non-existent net, said: 'Vodka and orange?'

I said that would be fine. He smiled, the problem was solved. He turned away and came back almost immediately with the drink.

I said, 'You a gatecrasher like me?'

He nodded vigorously and said, 'I . . . *own* the house.' His hand waved. 'These people, ah, well, friends of my daughter I think, been here all weekend. Yeah . . . ah . . . yeah . . . come from all over. What about you?'

'I'm from England.'

More nods were forthcoming. He told me there was going to be an election in England soon. He was very confident about it. He knew someone who knew someone in the Thatcher cabinet. He seemed well informed about the British scene. He asked if I knew what was happening with the redevelopment of the London docklands. He said the whole deal was being arranged by a consortium of Los Angeles lawyers. He said, 'Downtown . . . lots of dollars . . . ah . . . *billions* of dollars . . . they're running the whole ballgame . . . ah . . . and . . .'

He halted in mid-stutter, frowning, as if he'd been caught in the act of donating state secrets to an enemy power. 'Someone else English here . . . from London I think . . . take you over.'

There was a sound like an approaching hurricane and the house began to shake and rattle. I thought it must be an earthquake. Los Angeles was famous for them. I tried to remember what to do. I'd read an article. Something about covering the head and crawling under the stairs. Or was that in the event of a nuclear strike? I threw myself on the floor and wrapped my arms round my head. The rattling stopped, everything went quiet, and I heard a voice saying, 'Ah . . . Amtrak . . .

train ... right outside ... every twenty minutes ... always shakes people up ...'

The man like James Stewart introduced me to a woman. She had big eyes and a square jaw. She was dressed entirely in red leather. She sipped a margarita and creaked as she raised the glass to her lips. The man said, 'You two ... ah ... the *English* connection,' and beat an anxious, sneaker-shod retreat.

'Nice leather,' I said. 'You're from London?'

'No,' she said.

I laughed nervously, as if at a private joke.

'But I'm going there. In two weeks. I heard you could meet famous people there.'

'And that's what you want to do?'

'Oh, sure.'

She explained. She had something called the GLQ, a.k.a. the Get Laid Quotient. She had it all worked out. She factored in how famous the man was on a scale of one to ten, balanced this against the amount of time the conquest would take and whether she would have to spend any money, and came up with a figure. She said Jerry Lewis was the least capable famous person she had ever slept with. I wondered what that meant, how would I rate? *Least capable*: it was a terrifying concept. By now she had moved dizzily onto another subject, and was saying how T-Bone Burnett was at this party somewhere and he had told her the Beverly Center was infested with huge killer rats and an outfit called Bugs Burger Bug Killers had been called in to deal with it. *T-Bone Burnett? Bugs Burger Bug Killers?* It sounded improbably alliterative.

She said, leather creaking and groaning, 'That girl Roman Polanski was arrested for, coke and sex in the jacuzzi, she's a big star in a TV sitcom now. I saw her sucking tongues with some guy at Carlos 'n' Charlie's. These Japanese guys were watching. Shouldn't think they knew who she was. They were talking about Pearl Harbor, probably.'

I looked round for Barbara. The room had filled up even more. People with gleaming teeth jostled for position around the tequila fountain. The man with the baggy shorts repeated his enactment of winning the jackpot at Atlantic City.

The red-leather girl said that she'd always wanted to meet (meet?) a real guitar hero, someone like Ronnie van Zant, or Chuck Berry, or Eric Clapton, or Jimmy Page of Led Zeppelin.

I told her I'd once met Chuck Berry. He wore bell-bottom trousers and a stripy yellow shirt and wouldn't let anyone within ten yards of his guitar case. 'And people used to say I looked like Jimmy Page.'

'You?' she said. 'Were they blind?'

The woman was too much. I wanted to throw my toys out of the cot. I wanted stimulants. I fought my way to the steel fountain and drank several tequilas. Then it was out of the sliding doors and onto the sundeck.

Barbara was there, with another woman. They were in earnest conference. This is the way they looked. Barbara was Barbara. The other woman had teased blonde hair and a short skirt. Her legs went on for ever. Kimberley, I assumed, and I sidled up. Barbara was remembering when the two of them were in Athens, staying in a hotel called 'Paradise' and sharing a room with a seventeen-year-old bigamist from Arkansas. She had three husbands. But things had gone wrong. She was with one of them and another appeared who was supposed to be on an oil rig in Alaska. She ran away to Europe, ending up, somehow, in Albania. The Albanians were going to imprison her but found out she was American and instead bundled her across the border into Greece. She became a nightclub singer, and was planning to marry a Greek shipping millionaire.

Barbara and Kimberley found the story hilarious. They roared.

'But what about the husbands?' I said.

'What about them?' said Barbara. 'How many do you think I've got? You think you're the only one?' Explosions of laughter.

Kimberley said, 'Remember that other time in Athens? With that very tall guy, wore blue suede shoes. He looked like a football player and came on to me in the elevator and *you* said . . .'

' "Are we going down to hell?" ' said Barbara.

More laughter.

'We went to a bar, then another and another. Some place where they had pictures of *goats* on the walls. And in the end, this guy, wasn't he English as well?'

'I thought he was from *Africa*,' said Barbara.

'I'm pretty sure he was from England. Either way, he passed out, right there in the street. We left him . . .'

'Went to a cop. Told him there was a *dead* man on the sidewalk.'

My brain hummed. Barbara went to get more drinks.

Kimberley said, 'My sister tells me you're an uptight, fucked-up Englishman.'

Thanks a lot, Kimberley.

'Only joking,' said Kimberley, laughing. She slid her arm round my neck. We talked about Barbara. She told me how Barbara had protected her when they were kids. If she was in a fight Barbara would come storming in, like Bruce Lee. She said, 'We've got to try and cheer her up. She's totally bummed about that movie part.'

'It was bad luck.'

Kimberley scowled. '*Bad luck*? Some bozo says "Fuck me and you get the part" and you call that bad luck? I ever meet that guy Joel I'll break his neck.'

Another train thundered by. The deck trembled. I was fazed. I couldn't get this straight. I said, 'The director told Barbara she could have the part if she went to bed with him?'

'She didn't mention it?'

'No.'

The man who was like James Stewart was out on the deck, shouting: 'OK . . . OK . . . Listen up guys . . . I'm sending out for lunch. Do you wanna do Mexican? It's up to you. Whaddyasay? Or will it be lasagne for 160?' He dipped his knees and stroked a careful backhand.

The insects inside my skull went onto overtime. The casting couch: I'd presumed it died with the studio system. Clearly, I'd presumed wrong.

We went to a place called the Quiet Woman Tavern. The sign outside showed a woman with no head, hanging by her ankles from a gibbet, thick splashes of gore pumping from her neck. I was surprised that kind of thing wasn't illegal.

The door swung to behind us, deafening the noise of traffic. There was heat and the smell of stale cigarettes. The bar was lit by lamps in the shape of galleons. Above the counter was an autographed picture of Richard Nixon, that square, putty-like face split by a terrible grin. The barman was an advert for lumberjacks: unshaven chin, red check shirt, black curling hair. I ordered beers, and heard Kimberley telling Barbara that I was not what she had expected. What might that have been? Slashed jeans and safety pins, a spiky haircut: ageing Sex Pistol? Armani suit and gold collar pin: city whizz kid? Tweed jacket with pipe and scarf flung round my neck: writer type? Or a public school boy, nasal vowels and bow tie: Rupert Everett in *Another Country*? It depended, I supposed, on the movies she'd been watching.

'English people,' she said, as I put the glasses down on the table, 'they're so neat.'

I was not fooled by this.

I watched a man at the bar. He had a backside that wobbled like the rear end of an articulated lorry. He hauled himself off his stool and waddled to the restrooms. I thought how few *genuinely* fat people I'd seen in California. Where did they go? Perhaps there was a state ordinance against obesity. Perhaps sleek, surf-Nazi police would arrive in the middle of the night, herd the fatties into cattle trucks, and dump them in Oregon. Or Nevada.

I said to Barbara, 'You should have told me.'

'What about?'

'About the film thing.'

'There didn't seem much point.'

'What did he say?'

'I thought Kimberley told you.'

'What did he say, exactly?'

'Does it matter?'

'I'd like to know.'

'Drop it, Richard.'

I had to say: 'You were tempted, weren't you?'

Barbara glared.

'Weren't you?'

She asked what I wanted her to say. That she had been tempted? That she had been on the point of fucking him and had held back? Did I really want her to say that?

'OK,' she said, 'I was tempted. I'd have killed to get that part. It would have meant a lot to me. I didn't do it, but I was tempted. Satisfied?'

There was a silence. Kimberley suggested it might be a good idea if I went to get more drinks. I walked to the bar. The lumberjack pulled beer into glasses. I asked about the sign outside. 'Well,' he said, 'I guess a headless woman would tend to be pretty quiet, wouldn't she?'

The sun was setting when we left San Clemente. Clouds bunched low over distant mountains, a hawk circled, pylons marched towards the twin white blimps of a nuclear power station, and four soldiers (crew cuts, beige uniforms, ears like pink jug handles) went by in a powder-blue Chevrolet that was like something from *American Graffiti*. I told Barbara I thought my sense of the erotic was derived totally from movies: the glimpse of Bardot's thigh in *Contempt*, Stanwyck's anklet in *Double Indemnity*, Dietrich and the cigar in *Touch of Evil*, Gardner's shoulders rising from the water in *Pandora and the Flying Dutchman*.

Barbara said, 'What sense of the erotic?'

She described a game she'd once played with friends. The idea was to call out the first word that came into your mind associated with water. This supposedly provided a guide to the subject's libido. In other words the right answer, the answer you'd want to give, was *bloody Pacific Ocean*, shouted very loud.

Barbara smiled. 'I guess if you played that game you'd probably say . . . *puddle*.'

Back in Los Angeles: Barbara and I didn't talk much. I was restless. It was weeks since I'd been near the Hollywood Wax Museum. I presumed I was fired. I asked McCrea for a few days off. He said this was fine. He also said his wife wanted to see me. She had news about my spiritual condition. I found this alarming. One afternoon I was up on Sunset. At the corner of Laurel Avenue an escape artist was shrugging off chains and padlocks, greeted by the applause of an onlooker, a squat man in a check sports jacket. The escape artist invited the man to chain him up, and the invitation was accepted. Five minutes later the escape artist was still wriggling. His efforts to shake loose the chains became desperate. A crowd gathered to observe his frenzy. The squat man grinned, revealing teeth filed to a point: teeth to terrify a barracuda. 'I know the trick,' he said, and walked away.

The phone rang in the apartment. A man said, 'May I speak with Barbara?'

I thought, *I know who this is*, even as I said, 'Who is this?'

'This is Joel Goldman at New World. Is she there, please?'

I thought about hanging up. I thought about telling him Barbara had come down with smallpox, emigrated to Bolivia, been gunned down by bank raiders. Barbara came from the bathroom, towelling dry her hair. She said, 'Who is it?'

'It's Joel Goldman,' I said, and handed her the receiver.

I could feel myself skidding. Barbara had told me I shouldn't be jealous, but it was no use. I couldn't bear to listen to this. I went out of the apartment. On Venice the sun struck sparks off the concrete pavements and flashed on car windscreens. A man with a chainsaw was giving the palm trees a haircut. I crossed the street.

It was five in the afternoon. The El As de Oros was jammed to the doors. The clientèle was young and mostly Mexican. Some roamed round the pool tables, holding their cues in the air like rifles, ducking down to smack balls into pockets; a group wearing black baseball caps and black T-shirts with a skull and cross-bones design on the chest stood by the jukebox, arguing; and others were hunched at the bar, as though stabbed to it. I ordered a beer, drank it quickly, ordered another. In front of me on the bar was a dish filled with squid. The sight of the rubbery, suckered flesh made me feel sick.

I asked myself about Joel Goldman. What kind of man was he? How old? How tall? Where did he live? What car did he drive? Where did he buy his shoes? What records were in his collection? I made myself a bet that he was an Eagles man, and imagined him in his newly built stucco duplex (Brentwood, Los Feliz?), jingling coins in his pocket, flipping 'Hotel California' into the still-under-guarantee compact disc player. I'd always hated that record. What did he want? I had a pretty good idea about *that*. How far would he go to get it? And how big was his penis?

'What the fuck do you know about it, man?'

This was a pool-table Mexican, swivelling his cue towards me like a sniper. He was short, with a pointy face and his hair slicked back. His forehead was beaded with clots of dark, dried blood. He continued: 'You seen a guy with a white suit and a briefcase, carries a .45, goes around saying "Call me Conan"?'

I said, 'Piss off.'

I thought: *hello, hel-lo, calling London, come in London, anyone at home?* Was that really me talking?

He said, 'You fucking with me?'

I said nothing.

He said, 'Don't fuck with me, man,' tapped me on the shoulder with the cue, and went back to the pool table.

The barman said, 'You were lucky. He thinks someone is trying to kill him.'

'Is someone trying to kill him?'

'Be a good idea.'

Back in the apartment, Barbara lay on the ketchup-coloured sofa, feet stretched on the coffee table, Tab in hand, watching TV, and I took a beer from the fridge, flipped the top, took a swig, let the beer cool my mouth, waited as long as I could manage, about twenty seconds, before saying it: 'What did he want?'

'Who?' said Barbara, all innocence.

'Joel Goldman.'

'Oh, him,' she said. 'He called to apologize. For what happened before. Said he'd been dumb.'

'Is that right?'

'Yeah, that's right.'

'Was that all?'

'He wants me to see him tomorrow. His place. Three o'clock.'

'Will you go?'

A shriek of laughter came from the TV. Barbara yawned and stretched like a starfish. 'Maybe I won't,' she said. 'And maybe I will.'

I was in the boot of Barbara's car, and I was uncomfortable. My head was crammed against a wheel arch, my legs were jack-knifed to my chin, and there was a sickly smell of petrol fumes. I'd put in a red and black travelling rug (just like the one I used to have at college) so my clothes would stay clean, and I held tight onto the thin-bladed kitchen knife which would spring the lock when we arrived where we were going, *chez* Goldman pre-sumably. I was sweating. My left knee ached. Three years ago I'd torn the cartilage playing soccer on a concrete pitch under the Westway in Ladbroke Grove. A pity, since up to that point I'd had a good game. Sometimes it seized, rendering me immobile.

The Mustang's engine was a throaty rumble and I thought: *what a strange movie*. Barbara had said, 'I'm going out,' and I'd told myself to be calm, not to ask where she was going. I had asked, 'Where are you going?' and she was silent. I had told myself not to say, 'You're going to see Goldman, aren't you?' and said it anyway. Barbara had stalked into the bathroom. At that moment I knew that I would go through with the plan. I'd formulated the plan the previous night, springing open the boot-lock with the knife, first from the outside, then from the inside. The plan was to find out where Barbara was going. The plan had a logic which I liked: Barbara would lead me to Goldman, I would thrash Goldman to a pulp, perhaps even use the thin-bladed kitchen knife.

I'd forgotten to bring a torch. Thin bars of light came in through the edges of the boot but I couldn't see much. I waggled a hand in front of my face. It was just a blur. Effectively, I was blind. Sometimes the Mustang's V-8 faded, the hiss of rubber over tarmac slowed to a stop (traffic lights? traffic jam? I could only guess) and I heard sounds. The sounds of engines: the chugging diesel of a bus, a rattle like a London taxi, a whine that could have been a Porsche turbo, a motor that wheezed and croaked like a dying breath. The sounds of the city: the convulsive honking of trucks, the steady whop-whop-whop of helicopter blades, a voice shouting, 'Try that one more time fuckwit and I'll rip out your eyes, piss in your brains.' An unexplained glomphing sound like wellington boots trudging through mud, and the sounds of music: 'Like a Virgin', 'Ballroom Blitz' and several bars of a Michael Jackson song I couldn't identify.

The Mustang leapt upwards with a crash, over a kerb, perhaps, and stopped. My head banged against the wheel arch. I heard Barbara's laughter and wondered if we'd arrived. I thought I'd give her a couple of minutes to get clear. I relished the prospect of confronting them, pounding my fists into Goldman's skull. Then there were new sounds: a click like machinery being engaged and a beating noise that began far away and came slowly, steadily closer. Thwock-thwock-thwock. Suddenly the Mustang was buffeted from side to side. My head banged again. My teeth juddered. What was going on? Was *this* an earthquake? Perhaps there'd been a warning on the radio, and Barbara had stopped to run for cover. Why then had she laughed? Barbara was crazy, that's why, she laughed at all sorts of strange things. The shaking was worse. I bounced up and down. The beating was very loud, *thwock-thwock-thwock-thwock*, and water began to leak through the cracks, a trickle at first, then a steady gush. *Thwock-thwock-thwock.* I thought, this isn't an earthquake, the dozy bitch has driven into the ocean, and I panicked, scratching frantically at the lock with the knife. It wouldn't budge. That's it, I thought, I'm going to drown. I was convinced. Then the sound seemed to be moving away, thwock-thwock. There was another mechanical click and it stopped altogether. The water slowed to a dribble.

My body went limp. I tried to guess. I realized. Barbara had decided the car was dirty. We were in a car wash.

I was hysterical with relief. I thought how it never paid to panic in these situations, how everything turned out all right if only you kept your head. I was about to continue with this dribbling when the boot opened. Light poured in. I blinked: Barbara.

I tried to move. I couldn't. I pulled myself up, then slumped back into the puddles in the boot. 'Oh, shit,' I said in a strangled voice. My bloody knee had gone.

'Richard,' she said, 'this is not the behaviour of a reasonable person.'

Patterson was at the apartment, in his leather jacket, sprawled on the sofa, reading the *LA Times* classifieds. His expression was smug.

I said, 'What's he doing here?'

Barbara said, 'You and me are going to Las Vegas. Patterson wants us to make a bet. $5,000 on the Lakers to beat the Celtics tomorrow night. I may even try a coupla hundred myself. Patterson says the Lakers are a certainty.'

Patterson says? It was the same old song. It was a nightmare. Patterson was grinning, stroking his beard and reading out loud from the paper: 'One night Flamingo, plus flight, $110. One night Golden Nugget, plus flight *and* jacuzzi, $150. One night, Dunes, plus flight, $99.'

He stared at me. 'Seems like the Dunes is the best deal,' he said, 'unless, of course, Richard wants a jacuzzi.'

What movie was *he* making?

The flight was only half-full. Somewhere between Burbank and Las Vegas I suggested that we could, perhaps, stay at the Dunes for two or three nights, turn it into a weekend trip, try and sort a few things out. Barbara said nothing. She had stopped talking to me. I tried to touch her on the arm but she flinched and struck me

in the centre of my forehead with a bottle of Jack Daniels. A nun
sat next to me on the other side, about forty years old with a
robust, bucolic face. Her name was Sister Theresa. I asked why
she was going to Las Vegas.

'God's work is everywhere,' she said, and stood up and
beckoned me to follow. I walked behind her down the aisle until
she found an empty window seat. She pointed at the desert below,
an alien landscape, red and desolate and cratered and infinite. She
said, 'Sometimes I imagine all the dead of the world rising up
through the crust of this desert and coming down like a plague on
the City of Sinners.'

The plane landed. Barbara and I walked in silence through the
marbled airport lobby. I saw Sister Theresa. She took quarters
from a plastic bucket clasped between her knees and shovelled
them into a slot machine, pumping the handle and muttering, 'Hit
me. Hit me in the name of the Lord.'

The cab was a Ford Galaxy, white, twenty years old,
suspension shot. In the back Barbara and I bounced like beach
balls. The driver had small, delicate features and his name was
John. He wore Ray-Bans and a dirty white cowboy hat with a
silver band.

'This is what I call real heat,' said John. That was what I called
it too. My thin T-shirt felt like a horse blanket. Barbara stared at
an enormous red and gold hoarding in the desert which boasted:
'We've got the fight of the millenium – Hagler v. Hearns'. John
said, 'First time in Vegas for you folks?'

I said, 'We got married here. That was a while ago.'

'Then this'll be your second honeymoon,' he said with a
terrible chuckle. 'Guess you guys'll be requiring a lot of . . . *room
service*. Huh?'

'Right.'

'You English?'

'Right.'

'I lived in London once,' he said. 'Met David Bowie.'

'No *shit*,' said Barbara. It must have been about three o'clock.
This was the first time she'd spoken in six hours.

It kept John quiet, at least until we were bumping down the Strip and he pointed towards Caesar's Palace, saying, 'Frank Sinatra tossed a table through a plate glass window on the top floor. Right there. Just 'cos a waitress spoke to him. She wasn't insulting him, or anything like that, just asked him if he was ready to order. It was like diamonds falling from the sky. The Mafia hushed it up.' He gave the steering wheel a sudden jerk to the left and the Galaxy went into a shuddering dive onto the Dunes forecourt. My head smacked against the roof. I asked if he was drunk.

'Hell, no,' said John. 'I used to drink and drive. Now I just do drugs.'

A sign at reception said 'Dunes Big Fight Buffet – All you can imagine! All you can eat! $5.95'. The bald desk clerk gazed into his computer. He was mournful. He said, 'I don't see how this can have happened. Your booking is confirmed. But the only room we have available is the bridal suite on floor twenty-five. That's generally $700 a night. I guess I have no option but to give you that. It's very irregular.'

The room was circular. There was an emperor-sized circular water bed and on the ceiling a circular mirror. The carpet, curtains, walls, sofa, chairs and imitation Louis XV writing table were pink. Barbara walked to the window and looked out over the Strip. I set down the bags, saying 'Here we are again. And in the bridal suite.'

She said nothing.

'Let's go downstairs. Lose lots of money.'

'You're going downstairs. I'm going to sleep.'

I said, 'Can't we talk about this?'

She turned: 'Go away, Richard.'

She locked me out of the room. She kept the chain on the door. It seemed a haphazard way to finish things, if that's what it was supposed to be. I was puzzled: birdless in Vegas, at the Dunes.

I walked down the Strip. In the fountain outside the MGM Grand plumes of water jetted from the nipples of bronze, naked women. The sky was bleached by heat and the air scorched my lungs. I stopped for whisky at the Silver Slipper. In the bar two Germans screamed and aimed head butts at each other. I drank a lot. By seven I was in the Elizabethan Steak Room at Circus Circus. It was gloomy, and meat crackled on spits.

A man asked if he could share my table. He was small and wore a canary-yellow suit studded with rhinestones. A tall cowboy hat bobbled on his head. He was the drunkest person I've ever seen who could still stand up. He rocked to and fro and his eyes rolled, disclosing the whites, as if poached eggs were cooking in the sockets. Without waiting for my reply he sat down and belched. His face was green. He belched again. I was certain he was about to vomit, but he recovered himself and ordered. A chunk of steak arrived, a Matterhorn of meat, and he cut this with slow, heavy strokes, guiding each forkful into his mouth with care, chewing slowly and with great deliberation. When finished he belched, ordered another, ate it, and then noticed me. 'Name's Vance,' he said. 'I'm an oilman. Just got back from Canada, spent three weeks hunting elks with my twelve gauge. Never saw a single darned animal. In Scandinavia they call moose elks. Dunno what they call elks. You understand that? Puzzling business altogether. You wanna go see the fight?'

'Sure.'

'Then let's go,' he roared. 'Bring me my mule hat.'

We went to a bar and had whiskies. I felt drunk. There was a big video screen at the back of the bar. The fight came on. An announcer gave details. The challenger was Thomas 'Hitman' Hearns and the champion was Marvin Hagler, who had recently changed his name by deed poll to Marvelous Marvin Hagler. This seemed reasonable. I thought about doing it myself. *Marvelous* Richard Rayner: it was a name to conjure with. 'Gotta take a leak,' said Vance suddenly and lurched towards the restroom.

The fight started, I winced at every blow, Vance came back. He said, 'What's the deal?'

I said, 'The champ's in trouble.'

At this precise moment Marvelous Marvin Hagler launched an attack of startling ferocity, pressing the Hitman to the ropes and savagely clubbing him to the canvas. Vance nodded: the champ was in trouble.

I said goodbye to Vance and walked back along the Strip. At three in the morning I was in a low-stakes poker game at Caesar's. The cocktail waitresses were dressed like Roman slaves. I called for whisky each time one went by, losing money in a steady trickle, and then won the biggest pot of the night by accident, too drunk to see that in a hand of seven-card stud I had a five-card flush. There was silent amazement. The old man sitting opposite licked his pale lips and asked if this kind of play wasn't, in some way, illegal. The dealer said nothing and pushed a mountain of chips towards me. I sorted them into piles of blue and red and orange. There was about $1,200.

News spread fast. I became a celebrity. I had lots of friends. There were prostitutes and buskers, but most just wanted to meet someone who had been touched by luck. A middle-aged house-wife said she had seen the same thing happen once before, and such a blessing came only from God. She asked me to make the sign of the Cross.

A man in black bought me a bottle of champagne. He said, 'The limey's so bombed he couldn't see he had five hearts. That's what I call a real Las Vegas story. Lemme give you a drink.'

His name was Tom and he said he was a musician. He was unshaven and his eyes were cracked with red. He looked like he had been run over. He lived in LA and came to Las Vegas each month. He liked to watch the people. 'This place is demented, exotic, a nightmare,' he said. 'And I can never get an iced tea.'

When the champagne was finished we found a table and drank bourbon. I felt light-headed. My mind was a can of shaving foam. I was smashed. I told Tom about Barbara. He said I'd have to think of a course of action. I said *he'd* have to do it. I didn't have the machinery. We agreed that women were a pain in the head, a pain in the heart, a pain in the ass. Whereas we were real shitkickers. 'Sex,' said Tom, 'it's a bitch.'

A whore came up and asked if we wanted to party.

'What kind of party?'

She said that depended: on what the boys wanted and how much they were prepared to pay for it.

'Suck and fuck,' said Tom.

'Your friend clean?'

'Clean? He's English.'

'$300.'

'That's too much. $150.'

'OK. But fantasy's extra.'

'My friend might want you to be someone else.'

'That's fantasy,' she said. 'That's $200.'

I was so drunk I could scarcely move. Each of them took an elbow and propelled me to the lift. We went up. We went along a corridor. Tom opened a door and politely motioned me ahead. He turned on the light. Both he and the whore produced Saturday Night Specials. 'Hey, those guns look very realistic,' I said, laughing, assuming this was a game. 'Were they made in Japan? Or Taiwan?'

Tom pushed me onto the mattress and demanded the money. He was very calm about it. The whore leaned over me. She rubbed her gun up and down, up and down, against my crotch. My prick hardened. 'Easy come, easy go,' she said.

'This isn't happening,' I said.

I lay by the pool in the heat. The clock on the Dunes gave the temperature as 117 degrees and the time as 12.03, and a man in a green Hawaiian shirt announced himself.

'Hi. Name's Mal.'

I pulled myself up onto my elbows. Mal was small and tanned and wide as a lorry. He looked a little like the actor Jan Michael Vincent and wore a red baseball cap that said 'Screw you'.

'Wanna hear something beautiful?' He didn't wait for a reply. 'I'm thirty-five years old and I'm a bond salesman from Dayton, Ohio.' He pronounced Ohio like it was Oh-*one beat*-hi-*at least three beats*-oh. 'Last year I was number one for the entire state. Pulled down over a hundred grand. And you know what? I'm coming blood. I'm actually *coming* blood. Every time I have an orgasm blood comes shooting out my dick.'

My eyes blinked against the sun. Mal stood over me, staring, expecting some confidence in return. I gurgled nervously. 'Listen fella,' he said, smiling, his teeth white and perfectly shaped. 'Only woman'd give me a blow job be a goddam vampire.'

Las Vegas, the morning after: it boiled, it came at me, it was full of men like Mal. I had another epic hangover. The iron hat was screwed on tight. I pressed my hands to my fizzing head and moaned, thinking about what *could* be happening. I could be in bed with Barbara in that all-pink suite on the 25th floor, enacting scenes from a sex movie. Instead she wasn't talking to me and I was prostrate in 117 degree heat, dripping sweat, listening to Mal. This was not my script. This was definitely not my script.

'Yessir,' said Mal, 'every time I have an orgasm it's like my dick's trying for a major role in *Texas Chain Saw Massacre*.'

There was an explosion at the hotel end of the pool.

'A gun,' I said, nerves jangling.

'Like hell it is,' said Mal. Everything stopped. The only sound was the boom of the PA, announcing Keno winners. A beefy lifeguard swooped down from his high-chair to investigate and it happened again: CRACK.

'Some crazy bastard's throwing bottles,' said Mal. He was right. Another was on its way. This one carried further and smashed on the edge of the diving board, glass pock-marking the water and splintering on the hot poolside concrete.

'I see him,' said Mal, and pointed. I spotted a figure way up on the thirtieth or fortieth floor. Its arm waved, once and then again and again, sending down more and more missiles in a long and terrifying arc.

Mal said, 'Gotta be a kid. Only a kid would do that.' C-RACK . . . C-RACK . . . C-RACK. People were running for cover and there was glass all over, twinkling in the sun. A woman screamed as a splinter pierced her bikini flesh. Blood petalled the concrete.

'Just look at that. Boy, what a mess,' said Mal.

C-RACK . . . C-RACK . . . C-RACK. There were more bottles and panic set in. Some were screaming, other pulled on shoes and dived into the pool. An old man stood paralysed, not knowing whether to stay where he was and duck the bottles, or run and take his chances with the glass.

The PA stopped announcing Keno winners and issued the droning sounds of Kenny Rogers singing 'The Gambler'. Mal threw his arm around my shoulder and said: 'God, I love this song. Don't you?' I began to laugh.

Security guards appeared on the balcony, struggled briefly with the bottle-thrower, and dragged him inside. 'I hope they feed that jerk's balls into the wringer,' said Mal, as men in beige uniforms appeared to sweep away the glass. 'I hope they really kick that guy's ass through his brains.'

'At least they got this bloke.'

'Whaddya mean?' said Mal. I explained how I had been robbed the night before, and how uninterested security had been. He said, 'You should carry a piece. I always do. Got my brother's .45 service automatic.' He forced his thumb and forefinger into a gun and blammed at imaginary poolside assailants. '*Make my day*,' he snarled.

Someone touched my shoulder. It was Barbara. 'I want to speak to you,' she said.

'Excuse me,' said Mal, tugging his baseball cap politely, and not bothering to move.

'I've made the bet,' said Barbara. 'And I'm taking the four o'clock flight to LA. You can do what you like.'

There was a splash from the pool. I saw Mal watching me, pushing the cap back on his head, grin widening.

I said, '*What the fuck's happening, Barbara?*'

The PA system resumed its roll-call of Keno winners.

She said, 'I'm going back to Patterson.'

'What?'

'I can't handle this. You've been behaving like a lunatic.'

The car boot? I'd apologized for that.

'What's going on in your head, Richard? I never know. I never know what you want from me. I married you and you're messing me up. Get real.'

Barbara ran back towards the hotel, Mal's gaze tracking her all

the way. He let go a long, appreciative whistle. He said, 'I'll tell
you something for free and that's this, buddy. If that were my
muff I know what I'd want from her.'

I said, 'Mal, you don't happen to have your gun handy, do
you?'

Patterson picked us up at LAX. He wasn't attempting to hide his
glee. In the sprawl of Los Angeles I was a dinosaur, a non-driving
Englishman. I had always felt that not driving made me colourful,
strange, different. Patterson's smile informed me of the error.

We were in a tailback on the San Diego freeway, six lanes of
traffic nose-to-bumper, inching up the valley. Barbara was in the
front with Patterson, tapping her fingers in time to the radio. At
the end of the song the DJ said: 'That was Tears for Fears with
"Everybody Wants to Rule the World".'

'Not me,' said Barbara. 'I just wanna go to the beach.'

They dropped me on the deserted pavements of Sunset, near
the hotel where Barbara and I had first fucked. Patterson said,
'I'm sure you'll understand why I can't give you a ride home,
Richard. Love to do it, but I've got a hoop game to catch. See you
around. Maybe.' I looked at Barbara, but her eyes were fixed
ahead. She said nothing.

I had to catch the bus from the other side of Sunset. I got caught
in the middle while trying to cross. I was beached for about
twenty-five minutes, traffic blasting by on either side, and
watched a man dismantling the billboard of Mel Gibson. The
sawn-off shotgun was still slung over his shoulder but half of his
head was already gone. A blonde driving a sky-blue Corvette
almost clipped my legs off at the knee but I got back to the
apartment in time to see the final minutes of the basketball game.
It was a rout. The Celtics lost.

PARTY, PARTY

I TOLD WALLACE Moss about Las Vegas. He was neither surprised nor sympathetic. He laughed. 'Ba-ba-ba, Ba-Barbara Ann,' he sang, lying on the sofa in my apartment, peeling gum from the sole of an alligator boot, 'got me rockin' and a rollin', a rockin' and a reelin', Barbara Ann, Ba-ba, Ba-Barbara Ann.'

He said I should forget her.

Perhaps he was right. Perhaps the time had come to wrap up the whole deal with Barbara, chuck in Los Angeles, and head for home. That would have been sensible. Instead I picked up the phone, dialled the number of the house in Hollywood. Barbara answered, saying 'Ha-llo' in a tentative voice, and hung up as soon as I spoke. I tried again. This time I got Patterson. He told me not to call any more: he was going to disconnect the phone until the next day, by which time the company would have given him a new, unlisted number.

It sounded improbable. I thought how long such an operation would take in England. Two weeks? Four? Three months? I said, 'They'll never do that in a day.'

Patterson said, 'This is America. Goodbye, Richard.'

I called again. The phone had been left off the hook. And the next day I got a pre-recorded voice, saying 'The number you have called is no longer available, the number you have called is no longer available, the number you have . . .' Patterson was right. This was America.

I decided to try the Playboy Club. I walked to Pico Boulevard and waited for the Santa Monica Big Blue Bus. One came along. The driver was young, and wore sunglasses. I said, 'Does this bus go to Century City?'

He stared. 'No,' he said, 'I'm gonna turn it around and go in the other direction, just to fuck you up,' and did just that. I saw the other passengers make frantic gestures as the bus headed back down Pico. Another bus arrived. I sat next to a black woman who wore a thick, grey muffler and said 'Hot, it's so damned hot.' I wondered if Barbara would be at the club. I read the *LA Times*. A sixteen-year-old girl had burned her entire collection of rock-'n'-roll records on the lawn in front of the Mormon temple on Santa Monica Boulevard, explaining 'This music makes me feel lustful. It must be destroyed. Otherwise I will burn in hell.' Another story told how a transient carrying the credentials of an English journalist had been run over by a garbage truck while he slept in an alley in Mar Vista. How had they known he was a transient? Probably he *was* an English journalist. That seemed to be the way they treated English journalists over here.

At the Playboy Club the red-faced doorman with the dreadful hairpiece was gloomy. I had no time for his moods. I asked if Barbara was there. He said, 'She's gone. All the beautiful bunnies have gone.' I assumed this was part of a conspiracy.

I said, 'What do you mean?'

'It's all over. No more $20 tips from the Bunny Mother. No more shooting the breeze with Broadway Joe.' His voice was desperate, and he tugged at the lapels of his maroon jacket, rearranged the wayward frills on his soiled dress shirt, gestures whose meaning could only be revealed by extensive trepanning. He seemed about to burst into tears.

I walked through the lobby. A man wearing blue shorts and thick white socks with the rabbit-head logo wrestled with a life-size placard of Mel Torme. The souvenir case was empty, and there was the whiff of sawdust and the noise of power drills. Perhaps they were redecorating.

Lorraine was at the bar. Her peroxide hair was clipped short and she sloshed measures from different bottles into the same glass. ' 'Allo, Richard,' she said, in a thick, drunken voice.

'What's going on?'

'Club's closing down. Aintchu 'eard?'

'What?'

'Been losing money for years, so they say.' She gulped the drink and coughed. 'End of an error and all that.' Squads arrived and began to roll up the carpet that was the colour of left-over mustard. The Playboy Club was, actually, closing down. I couldn't quite believe it.

'I'm looking for Barbara.'

'I 'eard what 'appened,' said Lorraine, peering at a bottle of yellow, viscous alcohol.

'Do you know where she is?'

Lorraine said, 'Chuck's just signed this group called 'Dangerous Curves'. They need a backing singer. I may be going to Japan. Be dead groovy. Meanwhile, I'm going to get off my bonce.' She sniffed at the yellow liquid and poured several inches into her glass. 'If I were you I'd leave it alone. She'll be happier with Patterson, you know.'

'Maybe,' I said. If only he weren't so like a character in a Russian novel. The phone on the bar rang. It was for Lorraine. As I left I heard her say: 'Right, Chuck.'

I caught the bus to Hollywood. It was windy, the sky was grey and oppressive. I walked up the hill. Fat drops of rain splashed on my face and an empty Pepsi can clattered on the pavement. I was breathless when I came to the house. I knocked on the door. No one answered, so I crossed the street and waited under a pineapple-top palm tree. Water dripped through the leaves. A man in a sweat-shirt was at the window of the house next to

Barbara and Patterson's, looking down. What was on his mind? His eyes met my own, and he disappeared. I remembered a wet, summer day in London when I'd spent the entire afternoon riding the loop on the Circle Line, drinking tea in the platform café at Liverpool Street, thinking of Barbara and the way she looked. I remembered the first afternoon at the Playboy Club, watching the man with the purple lips, feeling the sweat on Barbara's back as she knelt to kiss me.

I felt tired and fuzzy. The rain turned abruptly to a tropical downpour, splashing knee-high off the pavements, and within seconds I was drenched, my cheeks flushed by the beating rain. A red and white ball swam past in the gutter. Barbara had once told me she'd seen a jacuzzi tub spinning down the street after a particularly bad storm. I heard a siren.

A police car came up, flashing blue and red lights, windows pearled by the rain, and a voice commanded, 'Stay right where you are, *don't* move, keep your hands where I can see them.' It was just like *Dragnet*.

A cop got out of the car. He was in his fifties, wizened and gnome-like, cloaked in a glistening mackintosh. 'OK, pal,' he said. 'Spread those legs, lean over the hood.' I pressed my face to the wet, hot metal. His hands explored: under my arms, round my chest and waist, down my hips and the inside of my thighs. He said, 'You wanna tell me what you're doing?'

'I'm waiting for someone.' I nodded in the direction of the house. 'She lives up there.'

'Get up,' he said. 'You from out of town?'

He sighed, took a handkerchief from his trousers, blew into it, and inspected the contents. 'Last week a guy who lives in one of these houses shot a kid,' he said. 'Fact was, the kid was lost, trying to find his way back to Hollywood. Guy thought he was a burglar. Guy said he felt real bad about it.'

That night I was feverish and wheezy. I shivered and I'd a bad headache. It must have been the rain. With one thing and another, it hadn't been what I'd call a successful day. I saw no way to contrive a meeting with Barbara. I was stymied. Then, later in the week, I got a phone call from an East German called Peter Schneider. He had met Barbara about a month before and she had given him this number. 'I also go out with a bunny girl,' he said, casually, as though all Europeans did. Why else would they come to America?

We met in the El As de Oros. Schneider was a sight. Bean-pole thin, nearly seven feet tall, he wore a New York Mets cap and had frizzy, rust-coloured hair. He spoke in a quick, clipped voice that was like a football rattle. 'You look terrible, you look like a sick man,' he said.

'I am a sick man.'

'And I am learning to be an American. This is also difficult.'

Schneider had been in Los Angeles for only six weeks. Back in East Germany he had written to one of the state newspapers denouncing the Communist regime. This prompted a visit from a member of the secret police and he was given a choice: publish a retraction, or go to jail. He didn't publish the retraction. He said, 'You see that movie *Midnight Express*? Jail was just like this. Violence. Sexual abuse. It is lucky I used to box.' At this juncture Schneider, a giant with a Harpo Marx haircut, flicked punches in the air, just to emphasize his point. Pool-table Mexicans watched the performance with amazement. He said the West Germans had paid for his release. He had been worth 50,000 Deutschmarks.

He said, 'I have this problem with Americans.' His voice was very loud. 'This big problem. They have no sense of humour. You notice this? It is obvious, I think. And no humorous writers.'

This was a bit strong, I thought, coming from an East German. I said, 'What about S. J. Perelman? Thurber, Roth? And Dorothy Parker?'

'Shut up, young man,' he boomed.

I calculated I was five years older than him.

'The woman was a fool. A complete fool. And another thing about Americans. So provincial. One time I ask Beth-Ann, she is my bunny girl, I ask if she had ever been to Europe. She said, "Never have. Never will. Too close to Russia." So what about Alaska? Incredible. Still she has invited me to this party.'

'What party's that?'

'For the closing of the Playboy Club. You know of this?'

There was a closing party for the club? I said, 'Barbara must be keeping it secret. A surprise.'

'Sure. All the bunnies will be there. Drink. Food. Video games.' These women with the floppy ears, said Schneider, they had plenty to recommend them.

I agreed. I couldn't believe my luck. But I had to wait. The party was in six days' time.

Norris told me a story. He had been at a surprise party for a lawyer in Pasadena. There had been a fight, one man pulled a gun and shot another dead. Some of the guests at the party were so shocked, so outraged, so *mad*, that instead of waiting open-mouthed until the police arrived they swarmed round the killer, disarmed him and tied his hands with a red leather belt. Then they took him into the garden and beat him to death with fence planks. They took it in turn, like Caesar's assassins. There were about thirty-five of them.

Norris said, 'This one dude, he was an out-of-work actor, turns to me and says, "I'm gonna call the cops and confess. My career needs the publicity."'

We were poolside at a derelict mansion near Griffith Park. Norris said the place once belonged to a big movie star of the 1930s (Garbo? Gable? Flynn? Davis? – he couldn't remember) before an arsonist got hold of a can of petrol and reduced it to a shell. The garden was overgrown, the palm trees charred and twisted from the fire. There was a smell like rotting food and an abandoned tennis court. Fat flies circled in the heat. I'd seen more cheerful places. Someone McCrea knew was thinking of buying the estate and wanted to know if the pool could be renovated. I stared at the cracked bottom, half expecting to see a corpse there, face down in the broken glass, bloated and decomposing in the sun.

I said, 'What do you think?'

'No way,' said Norris. 'Fucking pool's like the San Andreas

fault. Some bozo buys this place, cost millions to put it straight.'
He picked up a chunk of red brick and threw it into the empty
pool, sending a lizard scampering into one of the cracks. He said,
'You know that woman I like? With the red swimming pool and
the little dog? Chick cooled me. Got herself a new poolman, said I
was making the situation worse. Which was true. Threatened to
call the cops. McCrea was real pissed.' He threw another piece of
brick. 'You're the lucky one, dude.'

I explained about Barbara.

Norris rested a hand on my shoulder. 'Dude,' he said, 'you
must be totally bummed.'

I told him I'd been thinking. What had happened was not really
about me and Barbara and Patterson. What had happened was
about me and Los Angeles. I loved Los Angeles, it excited and
terrified me, and I'd prostrated myself before the looping
freeways, the creepy mansions, the renegade swimming pools
that turned to blood, the 128 assorted varieties of palm trees, the
stories of mass murders and fence-post slayings, the beach brains,
the surf Nazis, the dedicated careerists and religious fruitcakes,
the psychos on the bus. I'd just lain back, and Los Angeles had
fucked me up. I'd had enough of this. The time had come for
action. I was going to take Barbara back to London.

'Have you told her about this?' asked Norris.

'Not as such. I'm going to see her in a few days. I'll come up
with a plan.'

He nodded. 'Whole deal reminds me of a story I read in college.
Really neat story, about a guy from someplace in Europe, he's on
this train, it's back in the times of the old west, and the train has to
stop in a town because of a snowstorm. We're talking serious shit
here, dude – there's a mountain of snow blocking the tracks.
They're gonna be there awhile. So the guy goes into the town
hotel, starts playing cards with some of the locals. He's nervous,
he gets it into his mind they're gonna hurt him. The trouble starts
when he accuses someone of being a cheat. It's really a story
about Americans not understanding this European, he was a
Swede or some kind of Dutchman.'

'What happens in the end?'

'Oh,' said Norris, lobbing another half-brick into the empty pool, 'they kill the dude.'

Takowsky wore a blue linen suit along with his tan and glinting smile. It was a hot afternoon, around five, and we drove up Laurel Canyon, top down in his BMW, to meet an English director named Freddie who for some reason planned a film version of *Beowulf*, which I had never read and with which I had claimed intimate knowledge. 'This guy's *desperate* for a writer,' Takowsky had said. 'He may even take you.'

We pulled up in front of an ugly house of dark, grey stone. There were turrets and arrow-slits in the walls. It resembled a Norman castle. Takowsky said it was a Norman castle. A hand surgeon built it five years ago. He had an architect draw up plans and sent his wife to Europe, to Wales, to study the castles there and buy the stone. The surgeon had a corporation worth $3.5m and a male lover; actually, quite a number of male lovers. On her return the wife was informed and she hired a private detective. There were videos. So she got the castle, and was into co-production.

We walked over a drawbridge and down a crunching gravel path to a terrace beneath one of the towers where a crowd was gathered. A woman in a black dress like a sack came up. She was in her early twenties and her face shone. Presenting a burnished cheek for Takowsky to kiss, she gave me a look that said, 'Who are you? And what?' This was the video wife.

'That dress,' said Takowsky. 'Stunning.'

She said, 'Nick, he's the leader of my acting therapy class, he picked it out for me. He said it made me look like Joan of Arc. That place on Rodeo Drive with the fish tank.'

Takowsky went to find the English director. The video wife examined me warily. A waiter in white jacket and black tie arrived and presented me with champagne. The video wife smiled, restless eyes flickering to and fro, hand twitching at her hair. 'I only feel at home in a car,' she said for no apparent reason.

'Aaa-hah,' I said. 'I don't drive.'

'Then you shouldn't be in LA.' Her gaze slid over my shoulder. 'Oh God, didn't you just *hate* the Sixties,' she said, and walked away.

I wondered what I'd done to offend *her*. Perhaps she had taken one look and concluded: this man has no car, no money and probably no penis.

I walked down steps to a lawn which was bordered by hedges manicured to the shape of birds and littered with statues. There was a reproduction of Michelangelo's David (genitalia covered by gold spandex briefs), a Venus (naked), and a wax model of a woman in a white mini-dress and white boots, crouched over the handlebars of a Harley Davidson.

'That's David as in Goliath, right?' said a beautiful girl with blue hair and a bobbing pony-tail. 'But who's the bimbo on the Harley?'

'Nancy Sinatra.'

'As in Frank?'

'She was in a biker movie once, *The Wild Angels*.'

'Wow. Frank Sinatra had a wife who was a movie star?'

'Several. But Nancy's his daughter.'

She wasn't listening. She was looking towards the swimming pool where a man who wore a US cavalry stetson was vomiting into the deep end. He made loud honking noises. I'd gathered that there were various sorts of Los Angeles party. There was the filmster party where everyone knew everyone who was anyone and no one drank or mentioned sex. There was the sort of party Norris had described which erupted into sudden violence. And there was another sort of party, *this* sort of party, where no one knew anyone and everyone seemed to be insane. 'Gee, I hate these afternoons,' said the girl with the pony-tail.

A waiter appeared and refilled my glass. I thought I knew what she meant. I said, 'I've never been to one before. I'm from England.'

She laughed, the sound of tiny bells chiming. She said, 'I like England.'

'England likes you,' I said.

The little bells were again in evidence. She said, 'You dig punk music?'

'Some.'

'You wanna do some coke?'

This seemed a very good idea. I told her as much, and her black, dagger-length fingernails became deft and efficient, plucking a slim tube from the pocket of her bleached denim jacket and unclipping a small gold spoon from a chain round her waist.

'Here?' I said, looking round. The cavalry man was still honking. He was in a bad way.

'Sure,' she said, and we sniffed the coke. 'I really dig punk. Like U2. They're so neat.'

'That's not punk exactly,' I said, noticing a champagne bottle pushed between the Harley's seat cushion and Nancy Sinatra's wax rump. It was full, so I popped it and filled my glass. 'The Damned, I think you could say they were punk. The Stranglers were punk for about two weeks. And the Sex Pistols, of course.'

'As in Sid Vicious?'

'I saw them once.'

'You're shitting me.'

'In Huddersfield.'

'That in New Mexico?'

A man in a three-piece suit came up. The suit was all white and he wore a black shirt open to the third button. Chunky jewellery nestled among the pubic curls on his chest, and his mane of black hair was swept back from his forehead in a spectacular bouffant. He resembled an aspirant Bee-Gee. As he curled a proprietorial arm round the shoulder of the girl with the pony-tail, she said, 'This guy's from London, England, and he was practically in the fifth grade with Sid Vicious and the Sex Pistols.'

I said, 'The band was started by a bloke called Wally.'

The man wagged his bouffant, sending waves of after-shave in my direction. 'London. That's where punk music actually comes from, right?' he said, and laughed, a nasty, high-pitched sound which came up from the back of his throat and bubbled out of his mouth: *hy-erk, hy-erk, hy-erk.* 'I was there one time. It rained, the bars closed early.'

Thus, the English: a mob of rain-soaked punks who couldn't buy beer when they wanted.

'Isn't that Harrison Ford over there?' said the Bee-Gee, pointing to a tall, stooping figure. He grasped my hand. 'Catch you on the flipside, England, *hy-erk, hy-erk.*'

'It's been real,' said the girl with the pony-tail.

Takowsky was nowhere in sight, so I poured more champagne into my glass and set off towards the castle to look for him, passing a group which had gathered round the man who might have been Harrison Ford. I went through arched oak doors into a cavernous hall. Men in lime-green Robin Hood suits plucked at mandolins. It was gloomy.

'Freddie's finished,' said a voice. 'Freddie hit rock bottom three years ago, and he's still going down. Another year, the only thing he'll be directing will be the traffic on the Universal parking lot.'

Was this the same Freddie who Takowksy wanted me to meet: Freddie the medieval English man? If so, did Takowsky know that Freddie's career had become an example of the China Syndrome?

'What about Lautner?' said another voice.

'*Lautner*? He's just a dumb blond. He can be manipulated.'

I said, 'Excuse me. Would you happen to know where I can find David S. Takowsky?'

The two men seemed appalled by the question. They said they had no idea where David S. Takowsky might be. They had never heard of him.

I walked to the end of the hall, through a door and along a passage lined with rusty armour and shields mounted on the wall, wondering whether the surgeon had seen some particular merit in this architectural style or whether he decided to build a Norman castle just to get his wife out of the way.

There was a door at the end of the passage. I opened it. Inside there was a room with a TV set, a man with a ravaged face asleep in a chair, and another man sprawled on his belly, head propped on cupped hands. 'Ah hah, my *man*,' said this second man, 'come in, watch the hoop game.' It was Jack Nicholson, who was exactly like Jack Nicholson: round face split by a leering grin, and black hair receding from a creased forehead, coming to sharp points on his temples. He had on baggy khaki trousers and a navy blue shirt with 'kamikaze' written all over. I stood with my mouth open. Presumably he was used to people behaving this way. I thought of the movies I'd seen him in, the moments which formed part of my dream about America: discovering the flaw in Faye Dunaway's eye in *Chinatown*, jumping on the back of a truck to play the piano roped there in *Five Easy Pieces*, idiot glee and calling himself bad-ass ('Bad-ass? Yeah, I *am* a bad-ass. I AM a bad-ass') in *The Last Detail*. Why were these things so important to me? I remembered hearing a story about the worst lines he'd ever had to speak in a movie ('Be my sensible Susan') and was about to mention this when he said: 'Do me a favour?'

'Sure.'

'Sit down. And don't talk about the movies.'

'Fine.'

'Me and Harry,' he said, raising his eyebrows at the man asleep in the chair, 'we're not supposed to be in here. But they think I'm gonna miss even the first quarter of a Lakers game, they're nuts.'

'Who are they playing?'

'The Celtics.'

'I thought they played them the other day.'

Nicholson gave me a sharp look. 'It's a best of seven series.'

We watched the game. The Lakers, dressed in flashy gold strip, were winning with ease. Nicholson chuckled and from time to time stood up, roaring '*GO, LAKERS!*' When Worthy stepped to the free throw line he wriggled on the carpet, shouting, 'Do it, James baby, do it, my balls are in my throat.'

At the end of the first quarter the Lakers were ahead, 28–23. The Celtics were not despondent, however, and gathered round the team bench, leaning over a trim, black figure in a pinstripe suit who waved his hand as though instructing them to dig trenches.

The Lakers meanwhile were relaxed and full of confidence, laughing, slapping each other's hands. Nicholson said they always looked this way, even if they were losing, and said it was a cliché but sports teams really did develop a character which was an uncanny reflection of the area from which they came. Hence: the Celtics, from Boston, were grim, rugged and never gave up, while the Lakers were flamboyant and without self-consciousness. The Lakers had players who earned $5m a year and contrived to lose equal amounts in dubious real-estate ventures. On court, though, they moved like film stars: vain, moody, graceful, launching into improbable dribbles and scoring impossible baskets, playing in a style so outrageous and daring it seemed it might fall apart at any moment. Each game was a dazzling, vertiginous experience.

I said I had my reasons for not liking the Lakers. Nicholson found this unbelievable. He said, 'What's not to like?'

I told him how I had come to Los Angeles in pursuit of Barbara, how she had married me, how things had not gone according to script and fallen apart in Las Vegas when she had been sent there by her former fiancé to make a bet on a basketball game.

Nicholson rolled on his back and scratched his belly. 'Is this stuff true. Or are you putting me on?'

'It all happened.'

'My man,' he said, 'I do believe drastic action is called for.'

Afterwards I walked across the drawbridge and down Laurel Canyon. It was another of those outrageous Los Angeles sunsets. Behind me the hideous profiles of the Norman castle were silhouetted against a sky of orange and angry red. Mosquitoes the size of golf balls cruised the air. Jack Nicholson had set me straight. I had left without saying goodbye to Takowsky. I wasn't bothered. And I never did get to meet the Englishman who wanted to film *Beowulf*.

Schneider drove an orange VW Beetle and his travelling kit was laid out in neat piles in the back: sleeping bag, rucksack, towel, stove, tins of pineapple chunks, Swiss army knife, Gibbon's

Decline and Fall of the Roman Empire (in German, and in English
– the full eight volumes of the Milman edition), and the national
flags of both the Soviet Union and the United States of America. I
asked about the flags, and he smiled, saying in that staccato voice:
'Is it illegal to drive when deaf?'

I told him I didn't quite follow. He didn't bother to explain. He
liked to appear mysterious. I didn't mind. At last: I was on my way
to the other party, the one I'd been waiting for, the one where
Barbara would give in, become mine for ever. I felt good.

Schneider barrelled the VW up the curvy stretch of Sunset. This
was alarming. He seemed never to have heard of oncoming traffic. I
closed my eyes. Schneider was undeterred. He said, 'You have
noted the works of your English historian Gibbon? Los Angeles is
like Rome. During the reign of Commodus. Violence, decadence,
insanity. It is all here, and the sexually intriguing footnotes are not
in Latin. I have told Beth-Ann this. She does not like history. She
reads only Westerns. J. T. Edson and someone called Louis
L'Amour. Is that a real name? She loves J. T. Edson best.
Sometimes I think her mind is like the prairie. Empty with Duke
Wayne riding across the middle. You like the films of John Ford?'

'Some.'

'Your favourite?'

'The one about the PT boats, *They Were Expendable*.'

'Ah, Robert Montgomery,' he said, and went into a detailed
analysis of the cinema of John Ford.

My mind was elsewhere. My mind was on the plan I'd cooked up
after my talk with Jack Nicholson. Would it work? I'd tried to
cover all the angles. I was confident. And, after all, did Barbara
want to spend her life with a man who might have stepped from the
pages of Dostoievsky? The bottle weighed heavy in my pocket.
Wallace Moss had got it for me. He said he'd bought it over the
counter at Ralph's. Schneider was in on the thing. His VW was to
be the getaway car, if needed. He considered the plan quite
justified. He said, 'You try negotiation. If that doesn't work . . .'

Schneider explained that *My Darling Clementine* wasn't really a
Western at all, more a statement concerning the impossibility of

being a true individual within the capitalist system and turned the VW up a curving drive at the end of which was a half-timbered house designed to look like a Tudor mansion. This was Playboy Mansion West.

Beth-Ann met us at the door. She was small and dark, with disproportionately large breasts. She hugged Schneider and barely came to his waist. They were an incongruous pair. 'Who's this?' she said, looking at me.

'This is Richard,' said Schneider. 'He knows one of the other girls.'

'No kidding? Who's that?'

'Barbara.'

'I know Barbara. She's here with her boyfriend. The screen-writer.'

I said he was a particular friend of mine, and asked Beth-Ann if she knew where they were. She didn't.

I had suggested to Schneider we arrive early to avoid the crowds. This part of the plan was a success. There seemed to be no one there at all. We walked through a rumpus room with pool tables and pinball machines, which was empty. We walked through a room with a huge movie screen showing the titles for a film called *Babes in Baghdad*, which was empty. We walked through an astroturfed aviary, empty apart from cackling macaws and a bilious green parrot which screeched '*Fourth and inches, fourth and inches, give it to Marcus, go Raiders, give it to Marcus*'. We went through a room where a log fire crackled below an oil portrait of Hugh Hefner and there were a number of black leather chairs with no one sitting in them. It was the Playboy remake of the *Marie Celeste*.

Beth-Ann said she was taking Peter to the bunny warren. I wondered what and where that might be, and why wasn't I invited? 'Try the grotto pool. Barbara may be there. It's outside,' she said, pointing beyond french windows to a smoothly shaven lawn. 'Used to be known as the herpes pool. Now we call it the you-know-what.'

'I'm sorry?'

'A-I-D-S.'

'American women, so coy,' said Schneider.

Beth-Ann didn't agree. She butted him in the groin.

I walked onto the lawn. Here there were signs of life. A man stalked by, wearing flip-flops and a checkered bathrobe, pipe clamped between his jaws, escorted by a large, balding, cliff-like mass which chewed gum and was, I presumed, his bodyguard. The man saw me, waved, and I waved back. I shielded my eyes against the glare and went on.

The grotto pool was a frothing jacuzzi set among ornamental rocks. At one end was a woman in a black swimsuit and bunny ears, reading *National Geographic* and nibbling a chocolate bar, while at the other two grey-haired men discussed their physical condition.

'Spastic colon,' said one, pulling on a monstrous cigar.

'No shit,' said the other.

'Sliced me like a melon. Twenty-four stitches and each stitch cost the insurance $500.' He jabbed a finger at the livid scar which seamed his belly.

'Could be worse.'

'It *is* worse. I've lost my force.'

'I don't get it.'

'Sure you do,' said the man with the cigar, leering at the bunny girl, who reached to grasp another chocolate bar from a plate on one of the rocks. 'I'm having a little trouble.'

'Right, *right*. Can't they give you a pill?'

'I've been everywhere there is. Last week I gave a sample. Jacked off over a magazine in a cubicle with some nurse waiting outside, was as embarrassing as hell. They sent the tube to Bakersfield for analysis.'

'Bakersfield?'

'Beats me too. In a specially refrigerated truck.'

The bunny girl leaned forward, offering the plate of chocolate bars. 'No thanks, honey. I don't eat chocolate bars, I eat pussy,' said the man without the cigar, the one who wasn't impotent. He roared with delight at the joke. The woman forced a smile, revealing large and perfect teeth. What was it about American dentists? The man gave an appreciative grunt. 'That's what I call a mouth. Wouldn't that mouth look beautiful with two balls hanging from it?'

The two men laughed, horribly. I walked down a slope towards a croquet lawn and heard a familiar voice: 'Richard! What are you *doing* here?' I turned and saw Barbara, walking towards me from the house, dressed as she had been that first day at the club, all in turquoise. She appeared angry. 'How did you get in?'

'I have my methods.'

Her head flicked away, then she looked at me again. 'What do you want?'

I said, 'I've been thinking. I had this genius idea.'

'This has got to stop.'

'The two of us in England. Together. In London.'

'Richard, you're not listening.'

'So, you coming to England?'

'Of course not.'

'It's such a great idea.'

'How many times do I have to say it?' She headed back towards the house, stilettos snipping across the lawn. I followed.

'Listen,' I said. 'It's Los Angeles. It's been fucking us up. If we get back to England, everything will be OK.'

'It's not LA. It's you.'

'You hate LA. You said so. Remember? You said it was just a nightclub. A terrible nightclub.'

'At least it used to be a nightclub without you in it.'

'You can't stay with Patterson.'

'Would you tell me why not?'

'Because I love you.'

She ignored this. By now we were level with the grotto pool and I caught her by the shoulders, screaming: '*I love you!*' Now the statement got a mixed press. In the jacuzzi three faces stared, eyes popping and mouths wide. They were getting some entertainment. Barbara stopped and lowered her head, plunging the toe of a shoe into the turf.

She said, 'What am I to you, Richard? Your California beach girl? Your West Coast wahini? You never really thought about me at all. Did you ever, just once, stop and ask yourself what I was feeling? What I might want? Like hell, you did. Then there was your jealousy. How was I supposed to handle that? You're like a child. You have the ego of a baby. You're fucked up. You're a total fuck- up.'

I felt punch-drunk. Barbara was calling *me* a fuck-up. She had clearly gone mad.

She was marching towards the house. My resolve stiffened. Negotiations had failed. The moment had come for the plan: chloroform the bitch, kidnap her. Force was necessary. She'd asked for it. I watched her, thinking that if I could catch her at the moment when she opened the french windows then surprise would be on my side. I took the bottle from my pocket and unscrewed the top. I doused a handkerchief and a sweet smell like ether jolted my nostrils. I set out in pursuit, clutching the handkerchief behind my back.

I caught up with her when she'd already gone through the french windows. She was halfway across the room with the leather chairs and the portrait of Hugh Hefner. I lunged towards her, grabbing her by the neck and pulling her towards a sofa that was about as long as a cruise liner. I brought the hand from behind my back, pressing the chloroform swab into her face.

I'm not clear about what happened then. I'm pretty sure an elbow crunched into my ribs, and something fell on my head like several bricks. Then I was on the floor, in pain, aware only of the chloroform bottle glugging its contents over the sofa. I looked up. Barbara stood over me. Her legs seemed to go up and up and up. For a moment I thought she was about to grind a turquoise heel into my chest. I had a picture of myself on the plane flying out here, listening to a Greek policeman explain how even the famous leader Nikita S. Khrushchev had regarded Los Angeles as an earthly paradise. I remembered being fourteen years old in a school dormitory in Colwyn Bay, North Wales, where the windows always sheeted with ice in winter, taking my turn to masturbate over a photograph of Raquel Welch in thigh-hugging red shorts. I remembered myself aged seven, licking the sugary paste from the spoon which my mother had used to mix a cake hearing her tell me that one day someone would bake for me, just for me, every week. Where had it all gone wrong? Where was Jack Nicholson when I needed him?

Barbara leaned down and extended a hand. 'Get up, Richard,' she said in a kind voice. She hauled me to my feet and brushed dirt from my clothes. She smiled, and two things happened. First, Patterson entered the room. He looked at me with murder in his eyes and had a revolver pointed carelessly at my stomach. He was grinning, and had the appearance of a man who preferred to shoot from the hip.

'Richard,' he said. 'I'm gonna take you to the ball park.'

Then the second thing happened. The impotent grey-haired man from the jacuzzi came through the french windows. Characters were appearing like a scene in a drawing-room comedy. The impotent man sniffed, pointed his nose in the air like a hound following a scent and sniffed again. He chuckled. 'Hey, chloroform. I knew I knew that smell. Isn't that supposed to be a sexual stimulant?' he said and dabbed cigar ash onto the sofa. There was a *whoomphing* sound as the black leather exploded into flames. The man screeched, 'Yeah, let's *party*,' and I heard the bang of a revolver. I didn't know if Patterson was aiming at me, but he got Hugh Hefner right between the eyes.

There are 9,852 cells for the temporary detention of suspects in the Los Angeles area. At any time at least 60 per cent of these are occupied, that figure rising to 95 per cent during weekends and holiday periods when prisoners awaiting court appearances have to be bused from those precinct houses which fill up most quickly (Inglewood, Watts, Belvedere, East LA) to less crime-prone areas. Fewer than 10 per cent of those arrested are eventually convicted; the others cost the city a total of over $1m per day.

These facts were revealed to me by desk sergeant Carl Auerbach. Tall, slender, in his twenties, Auerbach had a mop of black hair and a drooping Zapata moustache. His expression was mournful. At high school he had been a star in the long jump, and an enthusiast of statistics. He said: 'Always was a numbers man, expect I always will be. I know facts about history, geography and politics. Facts about mathematical series and facts about the world series. Facts I wish I could forget. Easy facts. Hard facts. Soft facts. I can tell you the names of the books of the Old Testament, in order. The name of every president. DiMaggio's bat average for the 1953 season. Ed Moses' record for the 400 metre hurdles. I got a mind like a toilet bowl, this shit goes in, some of it sticks to the side.'

The Hollywood police station on Wilcox, eight at night: the scene was deserted and quiet, except for a series of furious, choking yells that came occasionally from deep within the building. Perhaps they were beating a suspect with lengths of rubber hose. Wasn't this what the American police were supposed to do? I couldn't understand why it hadn't happened to me yet. I also failed to understand why I had been neither charged nor thrust into a cell. Instead I was on a bench behind the front desk, wrapped in a blanket, seated beneath a row of wanted posters (desperate, unshaven, rat-like individuals – did I look like that?), asking myself why desk sergeant Auerbach was being so polite. Perhaps it was my accent. He said, 'You wanna hear the story of how they come to have those wooden Indians outside cigar stores? I got it from the *Reader's Digest*, about fifteen years .ago.'

I'd been there over two hours when the door banged open and Schneider came in. He was with a fair-haired man of medium height, dressed in a crisp tan suit. Schneider looked around, and spotted me. He explained that the man in the suit was from the British consulate. Schneider said, 'I have told him everything. What happened. How we make protest against treatment of women in the capitalist system. How it is just as bad as treatment of women in the Soviet Union. This is why we burn the flags.'

What was he talking about? What flags? I had no idea. The British diplomat meanwhile regarded me with distaste, making small, twitching movements of the mouth. He said, 'It was a very silly and, frankly, a rather childish gesture. What, might I ask, did you hope to achieve?'

I felt (I know) confused. I'd still no idea what was going on. Schneider was signalling with his hands. What was he up to? He said, 'That bump on the head. It has shaken you up, Richard. The flags we had in the back of the car. We burnt them in front of the picture of Hugh Hefner. Remember?'

Now I understood: I was a political activist, protesting against the degradation of women.

The British diplomat said, 'You're to be released. Very lucky for you that your friend had contacts at the German consulate. Very lucky for you that the parties involved wished to avoid publicity. Otherwise this incident could have landed you a jail sentence.'

I glanced at Schneider, wondering how he had pulled this off. His face was expressionless as he inspected the wanted poster for an escaped child rapist. Perhaps he was thinking of the mystery of life in Los Angeles. Or John Ford. Or Gibbon.

The parties involved didn't avoid publicity altogether. I think this was down to the curious mind of desk sergeant Auerbach. 'MILLIONTH HOLLYWOOD ARREST IS ENGLISH TORCH SUSPECT WHO DIDN'T DRIVE' said the headlines on page five of the *LA Times*.

British visitor Richard Rayner became the millionth arrest in the history of LAPD's Hollywood division this Monday, following a fire and a shooting incident at an unspecified Bel-Air mansion. Rayner, a poolman and unemployed screenwriter, was discovered by a patrol car at Sunset and Mapleton while trying to make his escape. He was on foot. 'I don't drive,' Rayner told arresting officers, 'but I certainly didn't mean to start a fire. I'm not an arsonist.' No one was injured in the incident and charges are not being pressed.

Takowsky rang before I'd finished breakfast. He said, 'Great move, Richard. Publicity never hurt anyone. Now you're beginning to get the idea. *That's* what I mean by high concept. With this I can get you meetings. Irwin Yablans will eat this alive. I always knew it. We're going places, you and I.'

'No, we're not,' I said, and hung up. I'd had enough. Now the time really had come to wrap up the whole Los Angeles deal and go home. I began to get my stuff together, and made a few calls. Norris wasn't home, so I left a message on the machine. McCrea said he was disappointed I was going since his wife Marlene still wanted to talk to me. I still found this alarming. He said they would remember me when they prayed, for the ball of redemption.

I decided to go cross-country by train, pick up a flight in New York, give myself time to think. Schneider and Moss lent me money for tickets. Revelationist Schneider told me he had spent most of the last month at Beth-Ann's place, watching videos over and over, and concocting a story plagiarized in equal measure from *White Heat, The Godfather, The Long Good Friday, Once Upon A Time In America* and *Prizzi's Honour.* He had sold this to Paramount for $180,000. He said, 'When in Rome, fuck the Romans before they fuck you, no?' Moss had a surprise as well. For several weeks now he had been running drugs from Los Angeles to Nevada, taping bricks of marijuana inside the shining new hubcaps of his Cadillac. I thought of the times I'd ridden in that car.

Moss said, 'You never did get a handle on any of it, did you?'

It was true. I tore down the map of Los Angeles and watched it burn in the rusted barbecue outside the house, smiling as flames gulped the squares of brown, yellow and orange. I'd known from the moment I was in the squad car that I violently wished to be somewhere else. The movie with Barbara was over, failed, flopped, *bombed.* Los Angeles: I wasn't sure what I'd got from it all. I remembered Auden's remark that there was more to life than fleeting emotions, that any marriage was infinitely more interesting than any romance, however passionate. Auden, it seemed to me, knew what he was talking about. I'd go back to Jane, if she'd have me. Stability didn't seem such a bad thing after all. Perhaps I was growing up. At least, I needn't have another adolescent crisis until I hit middle age.

Barbara came round that night. She wanted to pick up some

clothes she had left in the apartment. She didn't seem surprised that I was leaving.

She looked at me and said, 'I guess this is it.'

I said, 'I guess so.'

She said, 'I got something for you. It's in the bathroom. My dad and me were talking. I won't be needing it any more.'

It was the bunny suit. When Barbara had gone I pulled on the tights, then the corset, and the ears. She'd forgotten the shoes. Had Barbara's father told her to give me this? I could almost believe it. I was drunk. I was defeated. I was full of regret: Bunny Richard, goodbye.

The next afternoon Moss and Schneider drove me to Union Station. We went in the Cadillac. I eyed the hubcaps, and Moss assured me he wasn't carrying. My departure was marked by the usual bumper-to-bumper traffic insanity and another *Götterdämmerung* sunset. As we cruised Harbor Freeway, top down, breeze in our faces, the sky turned from a glowing nacreous colour to vibrant pink, and then orange and red. We swept down the exit ramp and I waved at drivers left behind in the jam. Aretha Franklin was on the radio and a billboard loomed over us. 'Wilderness Taxidermy of Glendale', it said, 'Stuff your loved ones.'

We pulled up in front of the station. 'So,' said Moss, as he took my suitcase from the back, 'next time you see me I'll have a silo in Kansas or someplace, just full of money.' I shook hands with Schneider. The three of us made the usual promises to keep in touch. It was all rather stiff and formal. Then they were gone.

The station was huge and dark, with a dull echo like a cathedral. The woman at the counter had purple hair and a mouth which opened and snapped quickly shut like a trap: 'Where to, mister?'

'That's all right by me.'

'What?'

'I said, "That's all right by me."'

'You jerking my chain?'

'It's a joke. Like the Carl Perkins song.'

'I'm gonna call security.'

'New York, if you please, one way.'

I took the ticket and walked to a news-stand. A black teenager in a yellow and green rasta hat went by, smoking a joint and muttering threats, and a *National Enquirer* headline said: 'Zero gravity turns rats to limp dishrags'. I examined the people around me in the station – the cops, the bag ladies, the transients, the jostling commuters – and felt pleased with myself. Perhaps I knew something these people didn't after all. I knew enough to get away.

'Please don't leave,' said a voice, and I turned, and saw Barbara. She was panting for breath, and wore running shorts and a black T-shirt. Her eyes shone and her forehead was dewed with sweat. 'I want you to stay.'

I was speechless.

She wasn't. She said, 'You'll have to change. We can't go on like before. I need you to think about me. I need you to treat me like a real person.'

I couldn't believe this was happening.

She said, 'I love you.'

'You do?'

We kissed.

I said, 'Give me a lift back to the apartment?'

'I can't. I rode here with Patterson.'

I felt dizzy, light-headed. '*Patterson* brought you here?'

'He's waiting outside. He's thinking of your interests.'

I stared at Barbara. How could she behave this way? My mind raced. A ghostly voice boomed out over the station, announcing the imminent departure of the Twentieth Century Limited to New York, and suddenly I knew everything would be fine. My mind cleared. I was gorgeously calm. I said, 'Let's get the train.'

Barbara gave me a puzzled look. I felt better by the moment and resumed, telling her we could sneak back into Los Angeles in a few days and in the meantime it would be an adventure, just like a movie: Hitchcock, *The Thirty-Nine Steps*, Robert Donat and Madeleine Carroll, handcuffed together, on the run.

I was Madeleine Carroll.

Illustrations by Huntley/Muir

Photoset in 10½/14pt Linotron Sabon
by Deltatype Ltd, Ellesmere Port
Printed and bound in Great Britain by
Billing Sons Ltd, Worcester